"How do you ___ ___ ___," he asked.

Her mouth grew tight in frustration.

"You should at least see the ranch's nurse. I can take you."

Zelda exhaled in resignation. "Thank you. You're right. And the sooner I get this looked at, the sooner I can start recovering."

Troy tapped her nose playfully. "Atta girl."

Her pretty blue eyes held his, the color of bluebonnets he'd seen during a circuit stop in Texas. Pretty blue eyes that had tempted him from the first time he'd seen her. Pretty blue eyes he'd done his best to resist.

Other than one impulsive moment when they'd kissed.

His mouth went dry, his heart pounding in his ears. He cleared his throat. "Now, hold still while I pick you up and carry you."

Her eyes went wild as she squeaked, "While you do what?"

Smiling, he slid his arms under her legs and behind her back, and scooped her up and against his chest. He shifted the sweet softness of her, her face only a few inches away. All resolution for a reputation makeover aside, he couldn't resist saying, "And yes, you can carry me next time when I need rescuing."

Dear Reader,

When I planned this three-sisters installment of my Top Dog Dude Ranch series, I knew that I wanted to include a child's journey to find a kidney donor, but I had no idea how personal the subject of organ donation would become to my family. As I wrote the second of these three books, *Charming the Cowboy*, my sister-in-law started the screening process to be a living donor. And she wasn't offering a kidney to a family member or a friend, but to a total stranger. I'm inspired by her heart, generosity and sacrifice.

I hope in reading this novel you'll be inspired as well to consider adding the organ donor designation to your driver's license. If you would like to learn more information about organ donation, check out organdonor.gov.

I enjoy hearing from readers and can be found frequently on Facebook, Instagram and TikTok. Links are on my website, catherinemann.com. Also on my website, check out my monthly contest giveaway and sign up for my newsletter for all the latest scoop!

Happy reading,

Cathy

Catherine Mann, *USA TODAY* bestselling author
CatherineMann.com

CHARMING
THE COWBOY

CATHERINE MANN

SPECIAL EDITION

Harlequin®
SPECIAL EDITION™

Recycling programs
for this product may
not exist in your area.

ISBN-13: 978-1-335-40237-0

Charming the Cowboy

Copyright © 2025 by Catherine Mann

 Harlequin Enterprises ULC
22 Adelaide St. West, 41st Floor
Toronto, Ontario M5H 4E3, Canada
www.Harlequin.com

Printed in Lithuania

MIX
Paper | Supporting
responsible forestry
FSC® C021394

USA TODAY bestselling author **Catherine Mann** is the author of over a hundred contemporary romance titles, released in more than twenty countries. Catherine's novels have won numerous awards, including a RITA® Award, the *RT Book Reviews* Reviewers' Choice Award and the Booksellers' Best Award. After years of moving around the country, Catherine has settled back in her home state of South Carolina with her Harley-riding husband. Empty nesters, they have a blended family of nine children, nine grandchildren, two dogs and three feral cats. FMI, visit her website: catherinemann.com.

Books by Catherine Mann

Harlequin Special Edition

Top Dog Dude Ranch

Charming the Cowboy
A Fairy-Tail Ending
Last-Chance Marriage Rescue
The Cowboy's Christmas Retreat
Last Chance on Moonlight Ridge
The Little Matchmaker
The Cowgirl and the Country M.D.
The Lawman's Surprise

Montana Mavericks: The Tenacity Social Club

A Maverick's Road Home

Montana Mavericks: The Anniversary Gift

Maverick's Secret Daughter

Visit the Author Profile page
at Harlequin.com for more titles.

To Kim Scott
Your generous gift of life to another is an inspiration.

Chapter One

Zelda Dalton's favorite fairy tale as a child had been *Rapunzel*. She'd even begged her mother not to cut her hair, no matter how much it hurt to comb out snarls after washing. Back then, the notion of rescuing herself, of being the hero of her own story, had filled Zelda with excitement and adventure.

Reality, though, was far removed from fairy tales right now.

She stared down at the broken brushed-nickel doorknob in her hand. Like her favorite fairy tale heroine, she was trapped. Albeit, not in a tower. Instead, she was trapped inside her dog-grooming salon at the Top Dog Dude Ranch. So much for letting a honeysuckle-scented breeze sweep away the scent of wet dog. Why did things like this only happen at the end of the day when she was sweaty and smelled of musty canines?

Her current client, a hyper golden retriever appropriately named Comet, whined and wriggled against the lavender leash restraining him to the grooming table.

"I know, Comet. I'm frustrated, too," Zelda called over her shoulder, furiously wrangling the knob back into the slot only to have it fall off at the slightest twist.

The sound of Comet scratching against the grooves of the tabletop echoed from behind her. "Just hold on a minute longer and I'll get you the very best treat."

A lock of hair straggled free from her long braid and she huffed it away, studying the door from a different angle. In a move Rapunzel would have applauded, she kneeled to peer through the tiny hole to the usually well-packed reception area. All she had to do was signal to someone, anyone. But instead of a flurry of activity, only an empty reception area stared back.

Surely she could figure out an escape plan on her own rather than embarrass herself by calling her boss. Her new job at the Top Dog Dude Ranch was too important to risk appearing incompetent. She needed this fresh start, a miracle, really. Her grandmother's last will and testament requested that Zelda and her two sisters fulfill a final wish by spending the summer in Gran's former hometown. Gran had even left them money to supplement summer jobs in the region.

The reason for that request still shook Zelda to the core.

While Gran was growing up in Moonlight Ridge, Tennessee, she met the love of her life as a teen. Someone before their grandfather, but it didn't work out. Gran got pregnant and decided to give the baby boy up in a private adoption. Gran's father had handled all the legal paperwork.

Her final request was that the three sisters find her son and give him the crystal ring that her first love gave her all those years ago. The heirloom piece was a beautiful amber gem in an antique gold setting. One that Gran had always put on when she told her fairy tales, insisting it had magical powers to create fantasy worlds, inspiring many of the stories she told them over the years. Tales that emphasized the importance of family above all.

Certainly, learning of a surprise relative had sounded like a miracle to Zelda as her niece Lottie's search for a kidney donor had so far come up empty. The one donor candidate they'd located had come down with mono, taking him out of the running for the foreseeable future.

Even if Zelda had struggled to save herself in the past, she embraced the chance to help rescue her niece.

A movement from the corner of Zelda's eyes gave her only a moment's warning before Comet wriggled free of the restraint and leaped to the floor. She straightened just as he lunged forward. He ran zoomies around the small space, taking tight turns in a skid that sent the trash can tumbling in the corner of the room, knocking the vacuum to the ground. Tissues and fur rolled free. He soared over the low half wall sectioning off the metal grooming tub, then launched back over again like a rodeo bull set loose from the chute.

Sighing, she pocketed the useless doorknob in her navy work smock and turned her attention to securing crazy Comet before he destroyed her little salon. She'd decorated the space with such care, eager to make this summer job a permanent one even after Lottie's transplant. To lock down a future in Moonlight Ridge, Tennessee, far from her ex-boyfriend. A creep whose name was better unmentioned. Like Voldemort.

"Comet, come," she commanded, her voice hoarse from the full day after a late night at a ranch sing-along.

The furry dog pounced, landing beside her and dropping into a pretty "sit," as if he hadn't just been all but hanging from the rafters seconds earlier. He stared at her with wide chocolate eyes, tail swishing along the floor tiles and setting the remnants of fur into tumbleweed motion. As she glanced at the wall clock with a rose relief pattern, her heart sank. Just her luck, no owner was on his way to pick up this fella for hours since the guest was on a Top Dog Dude Ranch trail ride. She had no other clients scheduled for today.

No one would miss her—or Comet—until suppertime.

Admitting defeat, she fished for her cell phone from the back pocket of her jeans. Hopefully, she could reach one of her sisters or another staff member to come free her even though the salon was on the far end of ranch, tucked behind the stables. There couldn't be worse timing with a large batch of guests arriving at the dude ranch, but she couldn't just hang out here all night. Except her phone wasn't in her back pocket after all. She patted the right, then the left two times for good measure.

Where had she put it?

Zelda narrowed her focus as she scanned the room, the words of one of Gran's fairy tales reverberating in her mind…

All that we lose turns up in unexpected places to reveal a secret to us.

As a woman who could lose her keys three minutes after walking into a room, the saying was a mantra Zelda practically tasted on her tongue. She dug through the wicker bin, wrangling de-matting combs and undercoat rakes, eyes sliding to the organizer where the various handmade shampoos and clippers were organized.

A box fan swirled papers on the bulletin board. Coloring artwork from her niece Lottie pictured the child with her mom and her mom's boyfriend, Cash. A printout of her sister Isobel's latest dog blog. A photo of her other sister, Neve, in a tree, nature watching during her research in Moonlight Ridge. Digging through the soft microfiber towel bin, then the themed bandannas she had neatly folded at the start of her shift, she repeated her lost-things mantra again.

No dice.

She hated feeling scatterbrained. In fact, she resented anything that dinged at her self-confidence after her hard-won independence. Leaving Atlanta and an emotionally controlling boyfriend hadn't been easy. But she'd done it. She refused to be conquered by a faulty doorknob and a rowdy golden retriever—

As if reading her mind, Comet shot to his feet and snatched her phone from between two bottles of conditioner. He trotted back toward her, cell held gently between his teeth.

"Thank you, Comet, what a good boy." She reached toward him.

The dog backed away a step.

She frowned and said more gently this time, her

throat scratchy, "Comet, come, please, please, pretty please."

He paused and she stepped closer, hand extended again. She moved slowly, so as not to startle him. Three inches shy of contact… Comet darted to the other side of the grooming table, cell phone still firmly between his teeth.

"Comet," she said with an exasperated sigh that croaked the more she talked, "I'm not kidding. Come. Here. Now."

The shaggy pup feinted left, then darted right in a game of chase that left her breathless and sent the box fan crashing to the ground. She slumped against the wall beside a collage of canine body language signs. Maybe if she just waited him out, Comet would approach her.

Three heavy heartbeats later, the golden ambled closer, closer still. And dropped the cell…

In a metal water bowl.

Plop.

She ground her teeth in frustration.

Her boss often said there was something almost magical about the animals in Moonlight Ridge—or in this case, devilish.

Shaking her head, she scooped her phone from the bowl and wrapped it in a dry towel, certain she must be seeing mystical events where they didn't exist. She needed to be more practical. She just hoped the device could be salvaged. After relocating, she didn't have the extra cash on hand for a new cell. Especially after the way her ex had stolen her last phone and left her to pay the remainder on the owed balance. Yes, she could ask her sisters for a loan, but she hated admitting she needed the help.

With each thought, each worry, the room seemed smaller, trapping her inside. Her heart hammered harder. Her breaths came faster, each shorter than the next as her chest went tight in an all-too-familiar feeling.

She had to get out of here.

Time to move on to another means of escape. She dragged a metal chair over to the only window, a long, transom-style pane that ran the length of one pine-planked wall. The odds of her being able to crawl through were slim. But maybe she could keep watch for a passerby and shout for help. *Shout* being a relative term for however long her squawky voice held out.

Zelda climbed on the chair and twisted the lock, praying this handle wouldn't break as well. But smooth as silk, the latch gave way. *Success.* She cranked the window open and arched up on her toes to peer outside. The chair wobbled. She gripped the window's high ledge to steady herself.

Just as the chair toppled sideways.

Her stomach pitched as she plunged, trying to right herself and miss the sharp corners of equipment in the tight workspace. She palmed the wall on her way down as she landed on her feet. Pain shot through her ankle and she collapsed onto the tile floor. Tears stung her eyes. She peeled back the hem of her jeans leg and...

"Ouch." Her ankle was already swelling with streaks of purple. "Ow, ow, ow."

Comet sprawled beside her with a whimper, nosing her arm in apology.

"It's okay, big fella. I know you didn't mean to misbehave." She stroked his silky ears while she thought through what to do next, her foot throbbing. "You're a good boy. Just young. Being trapped inside all day can make a puppy go a little bonkers."

He rested his head on her thigh and her panic eased, the room widening back to its normal size. Even though her ankle still hurt like a son of a gun, at least she could breathe through the pain. She could even feel the cooling swoosh of the fan caressing her sweaty cheek. Her gaze zeroed back in on the bulletin board with its fluttering images and notes tacked haphazardly above the desk.

A desk with a sheaf of paper tucked in the printer.

She looked from those pristine sheets to that narrow open window and inspiration struck.

Scooching on her bottom across the floor, she grabbed the full stack of paper before grappling for a marker. Her voice might not hold out for long, but she would be prepared all the same. She just hoped someone ventured out this way before long.

The dog wasn't the only one who needed to be free of this space before going stir-crazy.

"Harper," Troy Shaw cautioned his teenage daughter for what felt like the millionth time, "I need for you to stay put until I get home."

Reins in one hand, he tapped his earbud more securely in place with his other. He'd taken the job running the Top Dog Dude Ranch's summer camp, hoping to spend more time with his daughter, and for the most part, the flexibility of the position helped. On the other hand? There didn't seem to be enough free hours in the day to calm his temperamental daughter.

His palomino's head dipped, slowing from trot to slow walk in the sun-speckled dirt path as a black-billed cuckoo darted across the canopied path a few paces ahead. Even-tempered Lyra didn't so much as tense in her shoulders at the movement as she continued forward.

"Daaad, I'm not asking to go to a rave." Harper's exasperated sigh echoed through his earpiece. "I just want to go to the paintball tournament with my friends."

"Then you should have completed your summer school reading assignment for the week." Parenting a teenager was difficult enough with two parents. But six months ago when his ex had dropped off their daughter for his turn at the Christmas holidays, she'd never looked back. Paperwork had come with the new year, giving him sole custody.

How was he supposed to help his kid understand her mother didn't even want the most basic of visitation? She barely even answered Harper's calls. His heart ached for the pain he couldn't save his child. Daily, he struggled to walk the line between sympathy for his daughter and holding Harper accountable.

"I did finish the work," she said, no better at lying than when she'd been a toddler with a penchant for stealing cookies. Her voice still pitched higher during a fib. "Jane Eyre and I are now officially besties."

"Wanna take a test to prove that?" he asked, leather of his trail saddle creaking beneath his right thigh as he signaled Lyra to turn left on the path. Responsive as always, his mare stepped over the gnarled tree branch that marked the descent into the outer edges of Top Dog Ranch's main building. "I found a ten-question quiz online—one that can't be aced by reading the CliffsNotes."

"Wow, Dad." Sarcasm dripped from her words. "Way to bring the trust."

"*Trust* has to be earned," he said firmly.

Two squirrels raced along branches, chittering to each other. Lyra uncharacteristically turned her head and chuffed at the woodland animals, which sent the pair barreling up the white bark of an old sycamore tree. Gently flicking his wrist, he called Lyra's attention back to the trail. Another lazy turn on the dirt path and the gentle peak of the dog-grooming parlor came into focus.

The last thing he needed were thoughts of the infuriating—and gorgeous—Zelda Dalton. "Or in your case, Harper, trust needs to be restored. Need I remind you about skipping school? I could continue with other examples."

Harper sighed. "Okay, okay. I'll finish the assignment. Am I allowed to read outside or do I have to seclude myself in the attic like a regency heroine?"

"Outside—our porch or yard—is fine." He was exhausted from trying to think of all the ways she could twist his words to justify breaking rules. "If you want, we can take in the movie-picnic this evening."

"Sure. I bet they're showing *Bambi*," she said, her voice dripping with sarcasm.

He decided to ignore the tone for now. Best to concentrate on completing her summer reading. "I'll see you shortly. Love ya, kiddo."

She grunted something unintelligible in response before disconnecting. Man, he missed the days when she enjoyed tagging along for a horseback ride, rocking out pink cowgirl boots, brushing down the horses and asking a million questions about everything from the origin of hay to the reason we have two eyes if we only see one thing.

He missed her laugh. Her smile. Her determination. She'd changed when her mom left them, and as hard as he tried, he couldn't figure out how to right Harper's world again. For a man used to winning through sheer determination, this failure, on the most important front in his life, left him frustrated.

And deeply worried for his daughter.

He'd taken the summer gig running the riding camp at the Top Dog Dude Ranch to make himself more accessible to Harper—and to give himself a reputation makeover to secure the financial backers he needed to open his own rodeo training facility. After his divorce, he'd thrown himself into the rodeo circuit, riding hard, partying harder, and always, always protecting his heart.

A tap on the back of his head pulled him from his thoughts and he swatted at whatever bug or leaf whispered across him. But another brushed his head and he jerked around in the saddle to see... A paper airplane?

He ducked just in time as another one zoomed past.

"What the…?" He angled sideways in the saddle and grabbed for the paper missile as it tumbled downward, capturing it a few inches away from hitting the dusty path.

Frowning, he saw writing scrawled in the folds. Opening the lined sheaf, he read: *Help me. I'm trapped in the dog-grooming salon. Thanks from Zelda Dalton.*

He pivoted toward the cabin with enclosed kennels off the back only to realize at least a dozen more paper jets littered the ground like strange flowers blooming amid the dark green summer grass.

Concerned, he nudged Lyra toward the carved hitching post in front of the small cabin turned state-of-the-art dog-grooming facility, where he dismounted with a soft thud as his boots stirred the dirt on the ground. His mare's soft nicker joined the sounds of summer on the mountain—a melody of birdsong and cicadas echoing. He strode toward the grooming salon, picking up one plane after the other, messages on each pleading for assistance. Stuffing the planes into the back pockets of his jeans, he made his way to the window glinting in the late afternoon summer light.

"Hello?" he shouted. "Zelda? It's me. Troy."

"Troy," she called out, her voice hoarse and distant. "I'm inside. Trapped."

"Trapped? Did the dogs tie you up?" he asked in jest, knowing Zelda was quirky and had an odd sense of humor. He couldn't deny he found their verbal sparring engaging and irritating at the same time.

"It's not funny," she answered, the scratchy sound

to her words growing worse with each utterance. "The doorknob fell off and the dog dropped my cell phone in a bowl of water. I can't crawl out the window because I hurt my ankle."

All thoughts of sparring faded over the thought of her injured. "How bad is it? I'll call for medical assistance."

"No," she squawked emphatically. "It's just a sprain. I only need out of here so I can go home, get an ice pack and prop up my foot."

"If you're sure." He unhitched the traveling halter from the saddle and slipped it over Lyra's head. She stretched her neck lazily, a contrast to the urgency animating his fingers as he clipped the permanently attached leather lead rope to the halter's tie ring. Following Zelda's voice, he rounded the corner to the side window. "I'll get you out, and if I can't, we'll call in reinforcements."

"Thanks. The front door to the lobby should still be unlocked."

"Gotcha." He jogged back around to the front door, marked Pawsome Pet Parlor.

The heels of his boots echoed on the wooden floor in the quiet reception area, a modest space with rustic shelves containing well-ordered bottles of specialty dog shampoos. Green vines of a pothos plant suspended from the right corner of the room wound toward a door to the back, leaves framing a white-and-gold-painted sign that read "Where the magic happens."

He tapped on the panel, the knob resting on the floor. "Zelda?"

"Yes, I'm still here. Me and Comet." She paused. "Comet's a dog, by the way."

He resisted the urge to assure her he didn't think she had one of Santa's reindeer. "Okay, I'm texting the main office to let them know about the door, but in the meantime…" He tapped out the message and hit Send, then returned to assessing the door. "I think I can take the door off the hinges with the multi-tool on my key chain."

"Oh, okay." She sounded skeptical.

"I'm calling my daughter to check in, but rest assured I'll work on the door ASAP." He typed in Harper's name on his list of contacts and tapped his earbud to have his hands free for the call.

Harper answered on the first ring. "Yeah."

"Hey there," he said, twisting the first screw on the upper hinge. The utility tool wasn't a dead ringer in terms of fit, but if he went slow and methodically, he'd make progress. "I'm gonna be a little later getting home. I, uh, got held up. How's the reading assignment coming along?"

"Are you going to call me every five minutes to check?" She sighed before continuing, "Jane Eyre's mean headmaster, Mr. Brocklehurst, just got in trouble because of the boarding school's horrible living conditions."

He decided to ignore the dig. The first screw gave way and fell to the ground unceremoniously. He began work on the next, feeling more confident in his plan by the minute.

"Sounds like you're making progress. You'll be entering a paintball tournament before you know it." He wished Harper could understand that he didn't enjoy being the grouchy disciplinarian. He would far rather join in the competition himself, but he had responsibilities to his child. "I'm sorry to be running late."

"Well, at least I won't have to go to the sappy family movie night."

Was that a hint of disappointment in her voice? "I'll bring home supper after I finish. You can pick something on Netflix for us to watch."

"Sure. Thanks," she said with the teenage monotone of disinterest he'd grown accustomed to lately. "Bye, Dad."

The call disconnected before he could answer. He tried hard not to take her dismissive attitude personally as he shoved his phone back into his pocket, then loosened another screw. Squatting to the lower hinge, he adjusted his grip on the small utility tool and continued to work. The next screw spun out quicker than the last. Almost there.

"Hey, Troy?" Zelda called through the panel. "Sorry to make you late getting home to your kid. This is really embarrassing. I don't subscribe to the whole damsel-in-distress vibe. This was just a string of bad luck after a long workday."

One final turn and the last screw tumbled. Troy held the door upright, not wanting it to collapse and startle the dog locked inside with Zelda. "You can rescue me the next time."

"Deal." Zelda cleared her throat. "I hope you don't think I did this to get your attention."

He winced at the reminder of how he'd pushed her away a few weeks ago, assuming her friendly manner meant something more and telling her he needed to focus on his daughter. Zelda had put him in his place without hesitation.

He cleared his throat. "I'm not *that* egotistical."

Hefting the door aside, he braced himself for the inevitable bolt of attraction that just about leveled him every time he saw this woman. This spitfire of a female who somehow made a dog-grooming smock look smoking hot. The smock, which today read "Dog hair is my glitter" across the chest, accentuated her curves in a way usually reserved for Hollywood starlets on the red carpet.

He gave himself a handful of heartbeats to take in the sight of her as she sat with her back against the wall, a damp golden retriever beside her. Her brown braid was draped over her shoulder, a bit bedraggled, calling to him to untwine it the rest of the way around her delicate features. Her long, jeans-clad legs stretched out in front of her. And as he indulged in a slow glide look, his gaze stopped short at the sight of her right foot, tennis shoe off.

Her hurt ankle. How could he have forgotten her injury? He started to kneel beside her but she stopped him short with a hand on his elbow. A gentle touch. Simple. One that shouldn't have made his heart stutter on a beat. But it did.

Zelda drew her hand back. "Would you mind putting Comet in the kennel behind the front desk? His owner isn't due to pick him up for another few hours."

She pressed a hand to her forehead. "I'll need to use your phone to arrange for another ranch employee to meet him here."

"Of course." He passed her his cell and pushed to his feet, drawing in a breath of air that smelled lightly of vanilla pet shampoo.

Troy made fast work of securing the dog, a squirrely fellow, but no worse than a boisterous foal testing freedom in a paddock. Once the kennel door was locked, Troy turned his attention back to the woman on the floor of the well-lit grooming room.

Kneeling by her feet, by her discarded shoe with a sock inside, he studied her ankle, gently touching. The puffiness and streaks of purple made him wince in sympathy. He'd suffered more than his fair share of injuries during his rodeo days to know a serious sprain when he saw one. "This looks pretty bad. I wouldn't try to put any weight on it."

"I'll be fine. Once I get back to my cabin, my sisters can help me if I need anything." She looked toward the ceiling, where the overhead lights hummed.

"How do you plan to walk to your cabin?" he asked, her mouth going tight in frustration. "You should at least see the ranch's nurse. I can take you."

She exhaled in resignation. "Thank you. You're right. And the sooner I get this looked at, the sooner I can start recovering."

He tapped her nose playfully. "Atta girl."

Her blue eyes held his, the color of bluebonnets he'd seen during a circuit stop in Texas. Pretty blue eyes that had tempted him from the first time he'd seen her. Pretty blue eyes he'd done his best to resist.

Other than one, impulsive moment when they'd kissed.

His mouth went dry, his heart pounding in his ears. He cleared his throat. "Now hold still while I pick you up and carry you."

Her eyes went wide as she squeaked, "While you do what?"

Smiling, he slid his arms under her legs and behind her back, scooping her up and against his chest. He shifted the sweet softness of her, her face only a few inches away. All resolutions for a reputation make-over aside, he couldn't resist saying, "And yes, you can carry me next time when I need rescuing."

Chapter Two

Zelda took in the Tennessee mountains, stunningly dressed in summer green, a much-needed soothing tableau to distract herself from being pressed against Troy's muscular back. How had she gone from avoiding this man to sitting behind him on his horse, the scent of him—a mix of detergent and perspiration—tempting her with each breath?

Tempting her to see if that one, crazy kiss had been as incredible as she remembered.

When he'd scooped her up, she'd assumed he'd driven his truck. No such luck. At least the throbbing pain in her ankle kept her from drooling on his yummy, broad back during the short horseback ride from her grooming salon to the ranch's main lodge.

She cleared her throat. "Thank you for the ride. I'm sorry to put you out. I can call one of my sisters to pick me up at the lodge's clinic. Isobel will be nearby with her boyfriend and Lottie for movie night. They can take me home after it finishes."

Sucking in a breath of magnolia-scented air, she ignored the throbbing in her ankle. Though Lyra's four-beat walking gait was as steady as horses seemed to have, the slight knocking back-and-forth movement sent pain stabbing through her. A deep nausea settled in the pit of her stomach. She closed her eyes, taking another deep breath.

"We'll see how things time," he said. "It's really no bother. My truck's parked near the lodge. I can pass Lyra off to the summer apprentice in the barn and pick up my truck. By then, you should be finished in the clinic. And if you need to go to the emergency room, I can—"

"Shush. Don't invite that negative energy into this conversation." She couldn't afford any downtime at her new job.

Ahead, the tree-flecked path curved to the left. Oak tree boughs canopied overhead, filtering the light through the rounded dark green leaves and pine needles.

He chuckled before asking, "How's your ankle? It can't be comfortable hanging down like that."

"We're almost there. I'll be fine for a little while longer." She stifled a wince as the horse stepped over a log, jostling her ever so slightly before settling back into an even gait. Normally she would have enjoyed a horseback ride, free use of the stables being yet another perk of this job that she loved.

With a click and gentle guide of the reins, Troy steered the horse onto the left fork in the path. Above, sparrows chipped and trilled as they flitted from branch to branch.

Zelda shifted in the saddle, leaning forward as Lyra walked around a few rocks in the path. She did her best to pay attention to the way the supple white oak leaves stirred in the breeze. Anything to push the feel of his muscles out of the center of her mind.

The main lodge of the dude ranch eased into view, the sunset and mountain mist giving it a hazy aura. The stately lodge combined rustic and majestic into the perfect retreat. Everything guests might need could be found in one of the stores lining the little Main Street stretching beyond the lodge. The pseudo town square sported a large oval that served as a skating rink in winter. During the other seasons, the same central spot hosted bonfires, dances and small theatrical productions. She couldn't have asked for a more charming place to retreat from the anxieties of her old life.

He cast a grin over his shoulder. "You're a tough cookie, Zelda."

"Tough?" she responded skeptically. Hand drifting to her leg, the pain radiating upward from her ankle, she did her best to settle herself with a deep breath. "Sure. I guess." She was learning to be.

"Hey, the whole paper airplane escape plan was inspired. I admire someone who doesn't surrender in the face of adversity."

"I can see why that would be crucial to a rodeo king."

"I've taken more than my fair share of tumbles in the arena." He adjusted his white Stetson, his light brown hair brushing his collar. "Did you use my phone to text the nurse to let her know we're coming?"

"As ordered," she said, unable to keep the prickly tone from her voice. She leaned back in the saddle, adjusting her seat as the horse clip-clopped along. Gentle hoofbeats joined the sound of summer bugs. "Although you can still just take me straight home. I'm sure my foot will be fine by morning."

"You're welcome." He glanced back at her, the sun streaking over his handsome face.

"I'm sorry," she said, sighing. "Really. Thank you. The pain is making me irritable." As was her attraction to Troy at a time she needed time to heal after her past-relationship debacle.

She'd always considered herself an upbeat person, but leaving Atlanta had been harder than anyone would ever know. Tougher than she could admit, because the truth was so hurtful.

Before coming to the Top Dog Dude Ranch, she'd tangled her life up with the wrong kind of man. In the beginning, her ex had been so charming, every dream come true. Then slowly, he'd changed, isolating her from her family and friends, cutting her down with small insults. When she'd broken things off with him nearly a year ago, she'd thought she could reclaim her life right away. But it was as if he still had an invisible hold over her until leaving her safe world filled her with panic.

She had managed to extricate herself from the relationship, but still felt like a shell of herself. A fraction of the woman she'd once been. She ate, slept and went to work at the pet-grooming salon. But some days it seemed like she was just going through the motions of her life.

The only time she felt remotely alive? When she'd volunteered at the animal shelter giving dogs a makeover.

Her hours with animals grounded her and revitalized her all at once. She needed to remember that. It was why she'd been so glad for the dog-grooming work at the ranch. She hoped more time with animals would help her recover some sense of her old self.

And as much as Zelda needed to heal her heart, she couldn't forget the more important reason she was here at Top Dog Dude Ranch. Her niece's life could very well depend on solving Gran's mystery.

Troy knew he should just ask another staff member to give Zelda a ride home. Certainly plenty in the stables had offered when he'd passed Lyra over to the summer apprentice. But at each offer, he'd insisted he had the situation under control.

For reasons he didn't want to examine, he needed to see her safely back to her place. Maybe if for no other reason than to close the door on the persistent attraction.

So while Zelda was being examined in the ranch's clinic—located in the main lodge—he took the opportunity to pick up to-go meals from the dining hall's buffet. Grabbing a tray to fit all three recyclable cartons, he walked around the thrum of newly arrived guests who were taking in the food stations. A fair reaction. He'd felt that way too when he took his first boot-clad steps into the dining hall. Not only did the large windows let in swaths of daylight, but the smells of barbecue and locally sourced produce made his stomach grumble.

The lodge hummed with activity, normal regardless what day of the week. A fiddler and banjo player were picking away live music from one corner. A long table waited off to another side with games and puzzles for those who wished to stay indoors and commune after dinner.

Even in his short time here—less than a couple of months—he already recognized more than a few faces both from the ranch and the town. But then many residents of Moonlight Ridge had ties to Top Dog. The ranch's gifted landscaper and her sheriff husband waved a hello, sitting with a teen and an infant. The gift shop manager and her Christmas-tree-farmer husband filled a table with their friends—the school librarian and her husband, a local contractor. A bunch of little boys filled the table; he'd lost track of whose kids belonged to whom.

So. Many. Kids.

And he couldn't seem to manage one moody teen.

A clap on his shoulder pulled him out of his frustration. He turned to find the ranch's whitewater rafting instructor—Gil Hadley.

"Hey, man," Gil said, nodding toward his stack of to-go boxes, "I know we've been working you hard, but that's quite an appetite."

"I'm picking up food for my kid, too." Troy shuffled from foot to foot, dumping sweet corn into his daughter's to-go container. "And uh, for Zelda Dalton."

"That's nice of you." A knowing smile kicked into

Gil's sun-weathered face. "I heard she had some kind of accident? Something to do with her ankle?"

"Word sure travels fast. You look like you only just came in off the river."

Gil wore swim trunks and a long-sleeved water shirt that still carried a hint of dampness. "The Top Dog Ranch is a tight-knit group. Like a small town. Any prognosis from the clinic nurse?"

"The nurse is out sick. Doc Barnett came in to check her over now though." Doc wasn't officially employed by the ranch, but pitched in on occasion since his wife was the stable manager, yet another instance of how the ranch and the town formed a seamless community. "He was here with his wife and the grandkids."

"Lucky turn. Sounds like Zelda's in the best hands. How's she getting back to the cabin? Do you need me to track down one of her sisters? I think I saw Neve on my way in."

Once more, Troy couldn't seem to hand off the woman who'd captivated his thoughts ever since she'd targeted him with a paper airplane.

"Don't worry. My truck's here." He gestured to the tinted side doors that opened to the staff parking lot. "I'll get her settled in her cabin with the food before I go home. I promised Harper we'd watch a movie during dinner—if she finished her summer school assignment."

No doubt she was making a diorama of her "torturous" school environment with a Stetson-wearing headmaster on horseback.

"Kids are a lot of work. My hat's off to you for juggling it on your own."

"She's my daughter, and I love her. I'm doing my best." He rubbed the back of his neck. "Although looking at those triplet boys over there makes me feel woefully inadequate as a parent."

"I imagine the boss would say that here at Top Dog, we're all family and family is there for you anytime." Gil waved a hand, gesturing to the tables of guests, townsfolk and employees.

"I'm only summer staff, though, until I can get my training center off the ground." He took a few steps to the utensils station, Gil following close behind.

"Regardless of whether you're here for three months or three years, you're one of us now." He grinned, then winked. "And maybe we'll get to see you if you come back to visit our new groomer."

Okay. He needed to nip these rumors in the bud. He'd taken this job for a reputation makeover to attract investors for his training center venture. He also didn't need his daughter hearing gossip that might upset her already shaky world since her mother abandoned her. "Oh, there's nothing going on with the two of us. I'm just helping Zelda out—that Top Dog family spirit."

Gil clapped a hand over his chest. "My mistake. Thank you for being there in her hour of need. Like I said, the Top Dog family vibe is an awesome thing."

"And the food is top-notch, for sure." Troy patted his container of barbecue, slaw and corn bread.

The summer job working with the camp for children with disabilities came with food and lodging. If he

hadn't been planning on starting his own rodeo training center, he wouldn't have minded sticking around
this place for a while, decompressing from his unre-
lenting touring schedule and the disintegration of his
marriage. His wife had moved on. He intended to do
the same—without abandoning his child.

Troy stacked his containers in a large carry bag,
then gave a quick but polite nod. "Good to talk with
you. I'm going to check out the dessert line while Zelda
finishes up with Doc Barnett."

Gil hesitated answering for a moment so long that
Troy thought he might razz him some more about
spending time with Zelda, but instead, the rafting
guide simply nodded. "You have a nice night now."

As quiet settled around him, thoughts of Harper
filled his head along with more worries about falling short as a parent. He certainly hadn't had much in
the way of a role model with his parents. They hadn't
been physically abusive. He'd been housed and fed.
But they'd left him to his own devices as early as he
could remember. No family conversations. No guid-
ance. And certainly no praise or even criticism. Just
the complete silence from two people who did their
duty for their unplanned, unwanted kid.

He scanned the room full of families, taking in
their animated faces and hearing their chatter. A father teaching his daughter how to cut her barbecue
sandwich in half. A mother walking her child to the
games table to make a selection.

Being a good parent was about more than making sure his daughter completed her homework. He

needed to leave behind his bitterness about what his ex had done wrong and start improving his own parenting skills.

He set down the food, pulled his phone from his pocket and tapped out a text.

Sorry for the delay tonight. I have our supper. After we eat, I'll help you with the homework...

He waited for her answer. She lived with that phone in her hand. The text status changed to *Read*.

No response.

Okay.

He pulled up #images on his phone and searched for something affirming. He finally settled on a cartoon horse giving a big thumbs-up, ironic since horses didn't have thumbs. Would Harper understand he was trying?

The "affirming horse" image swooped into the cyber waves. *Read*. Three dots filled the screen like she might be texting a response. A feeling of success filled him like winning his first barrel racing competition as a teen.

Then the dots stopped. But the text field stayed blank.

Yet again he was reminded that he was in over his head parenting Harper. There was no denying he needed help. Because each day that passed, his daughter who used to give him hugs and dandelions grew angrier and more distant.

Zelda hated feeling helpless.

Wincing as the doctor gently wrapped her ankle

in an Ace bandage, Zelda shifted on the light beige exam table, the paper crackling under her. Even with her leg stretched out, her ankle had gone from throbbing to agonizing in short order, so much so that she bit her lip to keep from crying. Of course, no matter how gentle the doctor was in his exam, he was still moving her foot.

Although her restrained tears could also be attributed to the fact that she was beginning to realize the implications of this injury. How would she manage to stand on her feet all day to wash and groom dogs? The timing couldn't have been any worse for impressing her boss, and she'd been so hoping to lock down the job full-time in the fall.

She fought back the tears as she submitted to having her ankle wrapped. Whatever she needed to do to get on her feet faster. The small medical clinic was in an office off the ranch's lobby. Nothing complex, but well equipped to tend to basic injuries. With pristine white walls, the room offered a stark contrast to the log wall decor of the rest of the ranch. The quick-care clinic sported a desk with two chairs in front. Deeper in the room, an exam bed filled one corner and a supply cabinet stood in the other. A metal sign with an image of a stethoscope-wearing collie proclaimed Dogter in the House.

Having Dr. Barnett nearby—even in an unofficial capacity—was a godsend since a trip down the mountain to town could take a half hour, or longer, depending on the weather.

Zelda smiled through the ache as he secured the

wrap with a metal clasp. She gasped at a bolt of pain, inhaling disinfectant-scented air. "I'm sorry to have disrupted your supper."

"It's no trouble at all," the country doctor drawled. Somewhere around fifty, he had a casual air that set patients at ease with his blue jeans and calm confidence.

"Lucky me, though. I've heard all about you." Zelda pressed a hand to her chest. "I'm Lottie's aunt. She and my sister sing your praises."

"Ah, yes, that's right." He nodded, making the connection. "Well, that's mighty nice of them. I apologize for not recognizing you right away. You're the new dog groomer, aren't you?"

"For the summer, at least." Hopefully, longer. She gestured to her swollen ankle. "That's how I hurt myself—a mishap in the grooming salon."

"Well, it doesn't look like you'll need X-rays," he said before cautioning, "but it's still a mighty fierce sprain."

She exhaled in relief, the heels of her palms sinking into the cushioned exam table, paper covering crackling. "I'm choosing to focus on the not-broken part of your diagnosis."

"That's the spirit," he said, pivoting to the small desk to jot notes and pull out a couple of flyers, all the while chatting. "When you're back on your feet again, I need to bring our border collie, Loki, over for a good grooming. Meanwhile, though, we could use a recommendation for a deodorizing shampoo. He likes to roll in cow pies."

"Ew," she said with a giggle, thankful for his distracting chitchat. His bedside manner shone, for sure. What might her life have been like back in Atlanta if she'd felt as comfortable opening up to her doctor there about her isolation?

Standing, he stapled the three papers together. "Remember RICE—rest, ice, compression, elevation. You'll need to stay off your feet as much as possible for the next few weeks."

"Weeks?" she squeaked. Panic swelled and the overhead lights suddenly seemed far too bright. Her stomach knotted over the way her ankle could threaten to throw her whole life—her other recovery—off-balance. "I don't exactly have a desk job."

"The more you rest, the sooner you'll recover," he cautioned gently. "But I understand you'll need to move around. I'll send you home with an extra Ace bandage and some crutches. Here's a handout on pain-relief options and an icing schedule. Feel free to call if you have any concerns or questions."

"Thank you again." She folded the papers into her pocket, then eased from the table, tucking the crutches under her armpits. Her fingers tightened on the flexible rubber of the handgrips as she eased from the exam table.

Adjusting to the balancing act, she hobbled from the small clinic into the towering lobby. Voices echoed from the dining hall and the check-in desk, but her quick scan didn't find Troy. A stab of disappointment rivaled the ache in her ankle. It shouldn't matter if he stood her up, but it did. Too much.

Sagging back against the wall, Zelda scratched her

head right over those spots where brushing her hair had hurt as a kid. Her mom had sworn she was just taking care of her.

Concentrating on her breath, on the right now, was much harder to do with the pain of her ankle. Palms pressing into the handgrips, she put her energy into this moment, staying in the present. She focused on the laughter from two young kids hunched over an over-size coloring book at one of the pine tables. Listened to the applause after a triumphant, tangy banjo chord drifting from the dining hall.

"Zelda?" Her name drifted from behind her.

She hobble-turned in a far-from-graceful move to find Troy in the archway between the lobby and dining hall. Relief made her knees weak. She was thankful once again for the crutches as she took in the sight of him holding a large brown bag with a Top Dog logo stamped on the side.

"Troy? Oh, you're still here." She tried to keep her tone nonchalant, even as her breathing threatened to betray her. All the noise of the lobby muted again as she tried not to notice the way his lips curved upward into a smile. Those bright, crinkling eyes now the loudest thing in the room.

He strode closer, boots thudding against the planked floor. "Did you think I would bail and leave you at the mercy of calling for an Uber?"

"The exam took so long, I wouldn't have blamed you if you needed to get home to your daughter." She felt guilty for making him wait, when he'd always been clear his daughter had to be his priority. He really was a nice guy underneath all that cowboy swagger. She straightened from against the wall with a slight wobble. "It's not like I would have been totally stranded."

"There's no reason for you to wait around until your sisters finish with the movie." He palmed the small of her back to steady her, launching butterflies in her stomach. "You need to take it easy. My truck is parked right out front and I can drive by your cabin on my way home."

"If you're not careful," she said, smiling up at him as they made their way out front to where the truck waited in an employee spot, "I'm going to think you're a good guy after all."

"We can't be having that," he said with a wink, lifting the brown bag in his grip. "I guess this is an inopportune time to mention that I picked up some dinner for you, too, when I got orders for my daughter and me. I assume you like barbecue."

"Truth be told, I like the down-home, casual meals here." And the busy, large dining room was a welcome change from the solitude of her old apartment where her boyfriend had done his best to push away the rest of the world. "If I didn't like country cooking, I might need to find another place to work."

His laugh rumbled up to the rafters, full and uninhibited. Intoxicating in its abandon. Her breath hitched in her chest. She definitely needed to get a grip on herself before she climbed in the truck alone with this man.

Grinning, he shook his head and nodded toward the

massive double doors. "I'll put our meals in the truck, then come back in to help you out."

Memories of him lifting her up in his arms made her pulse quicken and her thoughts scatter.

No way would she be swept off her feet again.

He started toward the door and she called out to stop him. "Troy? I'll be a gracious receiver. But this time—" she paused to wave one crutch in his direction "—I'll get to my ride under my own power."

Chapter Three

Harper Shaw checked her smartwatch for the billionth time, shading the light to stay hidden in the early dusk. Crouched behind the heater/AC unit in back of their cabin, she wondered how much longer she should wait for her new boyfriend. Her only friend in this backwoods place her father had banished her to.

Wynn needed to hurry up and get here before her dad came home so they could head out undetected. Pulling at tall weeds, she glanced back to the driveway, anxious that she'd see the headlights of her dad's pickup truck. She'd wanted to meet up down by the river, but Wynn worried about her walking around on her own.

Dreamy sigh.

She could afford to wait a while longer. They should have a bit more leeway on the timetable. She'd sped through her summer school assignment and left it on the table for her dad to see—and hoped he wouldn't realize she'd copied off the internet. She'd stuffed pillows under her bedspread with her noise machine shooshing away by her bed. Essential oils puffed a lavender scent into the air. A fan propped on a chair at just the right angle.

She had a rigid bedtime routine because of sleeping issues. Her dad wouldn't risk waking her—the fake her.

Her dad had a no-dating rule until her grades were up. Why couldn't he understand she hated it here so much, she'd been about to run away? She'd been sneaking out past the barn with a full backpack, intending to slip onto a tour bus leaving the ranch for good.

Then she'd seen him. Wynn Oakes. A summer intern her age who'd signed on to help at the kids' camp with her dad.

That day, like this evening, the sight of Wynn made her tingly all over.

Harper moved the stem of the leaf between her thumb and forefinger, her heart beating overtime as loud as the thrum of the bugs from the bushes circling their house. And then she spotted him.

Wynn stepped out of the cluster of trees and the last rays of the setting sun shone like a melting orange Creamsicle. He was tall and lean, even taller when he wore that cowboy hat like now. His junior state champion belt buckle sparkled like the stars she knew she had in her eyes around him. He held a backpack in one hand and extended his other for her.

Breathless, Harper eased to her feet and sprinted through her backyard to meet him at the forest's edge. She clasped his hand, another shiver chasing after that first one. "I thought you were gonna stand me up."

"Not a chance," he said, his blue eyes twinkling.

"I got delayed because your dad needed me to stable his horse."

Panic twisted in her gut, and she looked over her shoulder quickly. "Is he on his way?" Then guilt piled on top. "Was he hurrying to get home?"

She liked the way his fingers curled around hers. Solid. Present. "Nah, he was rushing over to give the groomer lady a ride back to her cabin. Something about breaking her leg or her arm or... I don't remember what. Maybe a concussion?"

Wynn wasn't the smartest tool in the shed, but he was so, so hot. And he had sick rodeo skills, the kind that put even her dad to shame. Wynn was a rising star on the junior rodeo circuit and she intended to spend her summer sunning in his royal glow. "Where are we going?"

"I got a couple of desserts from the dining hall. I thought we could go see the movie. I brought a blanket."

She ignored the voice inside her that told her dad that would be dopey. Tucking a piece of loose hair back behind her ear, she couldn't hold back a smile. "I'd like that. A lot. What did you get to eat?"

He lifted the backpack in his hand. "Apple stack cake, like my mama makes."

Her mouth went dry at the mention of a homey parent, sending a cold wave through her body. And unlike the tingles that Wynn's bright eyes sent through her, this sensation made her stomach plummet. "My mom's a gourmet cook. She learned from their chef when she was growing up." She paused, lowering her voice. "In the palace. Minor royal, distant cousin."

All lies. But her mother had taught her all about lying and looking out for yourself. And right now, she wanted Wynn's attention all on her.

"Wow," Wynn said with wide eyes, "no kidding, royalty? Just…wow. Well, this won't be quite as fancy as your mama could make, but it's good home cooking."

Forcing a smile, she nodded. "Come on. Let's get going."

"Are you sure your dad will think you're asleep? I don't want you to get into trouble."

She liked the way he worried about her. It felt nice to have someone care about her feelings for a change. "He won't notice. He'll be too busy working on stuff for launching his training center."

Which meant she would have to move. Again.

Yeah, he probably wouldn't notice if she fell off the face of the earth. And if he did? So what if he punished her. Life had already "grounded" her to a summer in the middle of nowhere with the worst cell phone reception on the planet.

Zelda told herself that taking a ride home from Troy was no big deal. He only lived a couple of cabins past hers. It truly was better than pulling her sisters away from their fun. The last rays of the day bathed the mountains in a dusky glow.

And yes, maybe she needed a little more time with him, since inevitably he would revert to his annoying ways and that would make it easier to cut him out of her thoughts again.

Preferably before she went to bed and risked dreaming about wrapping her arms around his waist, resting her cheek against his shoulder.

Now, she just had to figure out how to haul herself into the front seat of his Ford F-350, a massive vehicle, no doubt for towing a horse trailer— Before she could finish the thought, he grabbed her waist and lifted her into the pickup cab. The scent of musk, leather and Troy wrapped around her.

Her crutches clattered to the ground as if in echo of her heart falling to her stomach. "So much for getting here under my own power."

His broad shoulders filled the doorframe. "You can prop your foot up on the backpack."

She nodded toward the sparkly school bag in the floorboards. "I wouldn't have guessed you to be a Swiftie."

"It belongs to my daughter," he said with a smile that faded into a frown. "She's supposed to be doing her homework tonight, and unless I'm mistaken, the book she's reading is inside that sack."

Zelda stifled a wince, then sagged back in her seat. Eyes catching on the rearview window ornament—a wooden cowboy hat with "World's Best Dad" carved across the brim. "But it's summertime."

"She has a couple of classes to complete over break." Troy tucked her crutches into the back seat beside the sack of food while she settled in front. He exhaled,

head shaking. "Last year didn't go so well for her ac-
ademically."

"Teenage years are difficult." She'd seen how hard
he worked at being a good father, another piece of the
complex picture of this man, and yet another element
that made him all the tougher to resist. "I'm sorry. I
don't know what I would have done without my grandmother to help me navigate those tumultuous years."

"You weren't close to your mother?" Pausing, he
shook his head and cranked the ignition, the diesel engine rumbling to life. "Scratch that. I shouldn't have
asked such a personal question. I'm just at my wits
end with my daughter and scrambling for answers."

Looking down at the halter on the floorboard, Zelda
rubbed an itch right over her ear, at the spot that had
hurt most when her mom brushed tangles from her
hair. Chest tight as she breathed in the leather scent
coming from what seemed to be a new show saddle in
the back of the truck, she nodded to herself.

Talking about her parents, even now after all this
time, gave her a pit in her stomach. "Mom and Dad
were incredible people with a heart for service. They
devoted their lives to teaching in underserved com-
munities and overseas."

"That sounds admirable." He backed out of the parking spot and drove slowly past the ranch's gift shop and
bakery/barkery, paw print signs on trees pointing out
directions, mixed with motivational sayings like *Stay
paws-itive. Anything is paws-ible.* "But I hear reservation in your voice."

Chest growing tight, she took a bracing breath. Adjusting the cool air pouring out of the vent, she stared out toward the walking path that connected the main lodge to nighttime venues and cabins. "They didn't have a lot of time left for their children. Our Gran was such an important influence in our lives. We stayed with her for months at a time. Gran was the one who gave us roots, a place to call home as our parents moved from one job to the next." Zelda rushed to add, "I don't mean to sound ungrateful. Mom and Dad loved us and instilled a thirst for knowledge."

She stared hard at a family meandering toward a cabin, a little girl of about five skipped ahead of her parents, whose hands were entwined. An easy, care-free scene. The kind that she still was growing accustomed to witnessing at Top Dog Ranch.

"I've noticed that trait in your sister. I follow your sister's blog about her daughter's service dog. Cocoa, right?" He paused until she nodded, then continued, "Your sister's creativity is impressive."

"Isobel definitely got Gran's imagination for storytelling, too. Fables and fairy tales were such a big part of my family's tapestry. My sisters and I even have fantasy nods in our names. Isobel, as in Belle. Neve, a foreign word that reflects Snow White." She grin-grimaced. "And I'm Rapun*zel*—*Zel*da. Get it?"

He reached to give a light tug to a wayward lock. "You've certainly got the gorgeous hair for it."

Heat rose in her cheeks at his compliment. She cleared her throat and steered the conversation away from fanciful talk. "So, about being close to my gran…

After our parents died, we all became even more tight-knit in our shared grief."

"It's good that you had each other." He nodded sympathetically and quiet settled around them, cut only by the low hum of country music through the speakers.

Exhaustion grabbed hold of her, lowering her defenses and drawing her deeper into nostalgia, not all of it positive. Gran's grief had been tangible over losing her only child. Isobel and her sisters had taken turns visiting her, trying to fill her days with distraction. Dividing and conquering had seemed the best plan then—it still did. But it also led to more distance, a disconnectedness, among the three of them.

There'd been a time she was close to her sisters, but not so much anymore. Life had sent them in different directions. Isobel to Montana. Zelda to Georgia. And Neve relocating within their home state of North Carolina.

And now they lived—at least temporarily—as neighbors. Their three quaint log cottages were perched in a row on their own private path, surrounded by pines. The individual accommodations for the summer had been paid for with money left by Gran.

When Gran updated her will just before she'd died, she was under the impression it was possible for each of them to take the summer off. Neve had started a research sabbatical—and had already given notice on her lease. Originally, she'd planned to take her sabbatical touring state parks in a camper, but now she was spending that time at the ranch. Isobel was a freelance writer, so she could work anywhere. And there had been a job opening at the Top Dog Dude Ranch for a temporary groomer, which had seemed like such a good fit for Zelda.

Thank goodness they wouldn't be under the same roof. She loved her sisters, but she also valued her privacy. Reintegrating into the world after her cloistered existence with her ex was tougher than she'd expected.

Her breath grew tight and she focused on the haven in front of her. Each storybook cabin sported a small firepit with Adirondack chairs and was encircled by a picket fence, the cabin name spelled out on a plaque nailed to the gate. Solar lights lined the walkways along with bright, floral landscaping. All were utterly inviting and a world away from her condo in Atlanta.

All the better.

The first cabin, Isobel's, had a wheelchair ramp, for Lottie. Then Neve's. And Zelda had chosen the last in the lineup since it was more isolated.

Actually, though, the ranch offered more privacy than she would have expected. Sure, the website made it look spread out, but she'd figured that was just marketing. She'd envisioned a resort, with the cabins all packed in close to the main lodge. This was a little slice of pastoral paradise, lightning bugs dotting the fresh night sky.

A movement snagged her attention behind her cottage. Two figures sprinted just past her picket fence, toward a walking path.

Troy slammed on the brakes and hissed beside her, a low curse slipping free.

"What's wrong?" she asked, alarm stirring. Could

someone have broken into her place? But they'd been on the outside of the fence, more like people jogging behind all three cabins.

He put the truck in Park and threw open his door. "That's my daughter with my intern. Wait here and I'll be right back."

And just that fast, her rescuer bailed.

Five minutes later, Zelda worked up the nerve to test walking on her sore ankle and promptly grabbed the crutches instead. Troy may have told her to wait for him, but he looked busy about a hundred yards away chewing out his daughter.

At least she assumed that was his kid and her boyfriend.

Regardless, Zelda didn't intend to hang out in the pickup waiting any longer. She hated feeling beholden to anyone. Especially to a man.

In the dwindling light, she made her plan, mentally walking the path from the truck to the three small stone steps that led to her cabin porch. The steps would be the hardest, but at least two skinny wooden pillars flanked either side of the porch in case she lost her balance navigating the stairs.

Yes, she could get herself out of the truck. It wasn't like her ankle was actually broken. Luckily, no one would be around to see her inelegant transfer to solid ground. Who knew pinecones and pebbles could be such a hazard?

A few painful, hobbling steps later, she pushed the gate open on her picket fence. Her little dog, Maisey, shot through the doggy door and raced down the walk-way toward her. How had that been left open? She kept Maisey indoors, especially after dark. She couldn't bear the thought that an owl would scoop up her little scrap of a friend.

In answer to her concern, her front door opened and her two sisters filed out, Isobel wearing an overlong "Cocoa the Caring Canine" blog shirt and Neve in a tee from the North Carolina university where she taught. While they all three shared keys for emergencies, she could have sworn they'd made plans for the evening.

"Hello," she called to her sisters, struggling to lean and pet the senior Maltese mix. "I thought you were going to the outdoor movie night."

Isobel rushed down the cabin steps, long hair flowing behind her. "Cash offered to take Lottie to the movie so Neve and I could have some sister time with you. We have a whole dinner set up inside for us."

Neve swept past and scooped up Maisey, who was perilously close to tripping her. "We called your cell but you weren't answering. Let me help you."

Slowly, Zelda navigated the steps feeling like the ugly-duckling sibling. "I won the Murphy's Law Award for Clumsiest, Most Embarrassing Accident." Once on the porch, she sagged into a rocker with a huge exhale of relief. "I would have called you to help, but I thought you were busy."

Isobel grabbed a throw pillow from the swing and placed it on an end table before dragging it in front of Zelda. "Prop your foot. I'll run inside and get some ice."

Neve set Maisey in her lap and took the crutches, resting them within reach against the logged wall before sitting on the porch swing. "What happened?"

"I locked myself in the grooming salon with a soggy dog," she said as she stroked Maisey's soft coat for comfort, "and when I tried to open a window to call for help, I fell off the chair."

Maisey nosed her sympathetically. Zelda cradled her closer. She'd met Maisey volunteering at an animal shelter. Maisey's previous owners had "suddenly" developed allergies after having the dog for nine years. Not so coincidentally, their "allergies" had started right about the time they heard about an impending move.

Zelda had taken one look at the heartbroken, overgrown pooch and scooped her up, stinky fur and all. She hadn't regretted the decision for an instant.

Neve tucked a stray lock back into her hair clasp, ever perfectly put together. "You were sweet to worry about our plans, but you have to know I'd have come running in a heartbeat if you'd called."

Zelda swept a self-conscious hand over her frazzling braid. "Well, the dog dropped my cell in a water bowl."

They all three had their grandmother's dark hair, but their personal tastes kept them from looking identical. Isobel had a casual, work-from-home vibe. Neve looked every bit the professional professor. And Zelda? She preferred her own quirky style, considering herself a boho free spirit.

The screen door squeaked as Isobel returned with two plastic bags of ice and placed one on either side of her foot. "Are you sure you only hurt your ankle? We should take you to the emergency room."

"I'm certain it's just my ankle," Zelda assured her, welcoming the cold that eased the painful throbbing. "Doc Barnett came into the ranch's clinic. Troy Shaw saw one of my paper airplanes asking for help."

"Yay, Doc Barnett," Isobel cheered as she sat beside Neve on the porch swing. "He's the best. But what's this about paper airplanes?"

Might as well get the embarrassing part out of the way. No doubt her dilemma would be common knowledge soon enough in this tight-knit little community. "My throat was getting hoarse from shouting—I was already struggling from that sing-a-long yesterday—so I wrote messages on sheets of paper, turned them into airplanes and launched them through the open window."

"Creative," Isobel said with an approving grin before nodding toward Troy's truck still parked just beyond the picket fence. "Now tell us about how you ended up hitching a ride with a certain hot cowboy."

Zelda shook her head. "Nothing happened. He would have done the same for anyone."

Neve tutted, arms folding in disproval. "And he didn't even walk you to the door. Rude, even if you weren't injured."

Glancing toward the woods where Troy had disappeared, Zelda felt compelled to defend him. "When we pulled up, he saw his daughter running into the forest with a boy—that junior rodeo intern, I think. Anyway, she was supposed to be home doing her summer school homework."

"Oh my." Neve pressed a hand to her chest. No doubt the professor felt there was no greater sin than skipping an assignment. "I hear through the grapevine that she's a handful. Before the last rodeo show, she used horse-safe purple hair dye on the mane and tail of her father's horse Lyra. Used sparkly glitter on her hooves, too. Apparently she thought it would be enough to embarrass Troy so they'd have to leave."

Isobel gasped, but Zelda couldn't squelch a hint of admiration for the girl's spirit. "Harper's having a tough time adjusting." Zelda chewed a fingernail. "I feel guilty for distracting Troy. If he hadn't been helping me, he would have been home with her."

Neve's lips went tight before she said, "From my experience teaching all those Biology 101 classes, I've learned teens are determined and headstrong. If they want to sneak out, they will find a time and a way."

Reaching toward the metal side table, Isobel picked up the green water bottle she took everywhere lately, drumming her manicured fingernails against the metal. A sticker carried a logo for her blog—and for the kidney donation registry. "Well, we're here, with dinner, ready to take care of you. The only question is inside or outside?"

"I don't want to be an imposition."

Isobel cradled her water bottle to her chest. "You've both already uprooted your entire lives for me and for my daughter. I can never repay you."

Zelda thumbed the silver spoon ring on her finger,

spinning. Gran had given them all three a similar ring as teens, but her sisters had lost theirs over the years. "I wouldn't want to be anywhere else."

Even if she hadn't been in need of an escape from her previous relationship, Zelda would have packed up her little VW Bug in a heartbeat to join in this quest. Her sister and her niece needed her. Gran wanted this. And Zelda wouldn't let them down. She would push through, one grounding breath at a time. Hopefully, the temp groomer's job at the Top Dog Dude Ranch would keep her too busy to think about the mess of a life she'd left behind. Or too busy to worry about how uncomfortable she felt about leaving Atlanta in the first place.

But coming here had 100 percent been the right thing to do—for herself and for her niece. "Okay, since it's such a gorgeous mountain night, let's eat out here on the porch."

Women on a mission, both sisters bolted from the swing and into the cabin, screen door slamming behind them.

Distant chords of a fiddle drifted toward them from the main lodge, twining with the call of crickets and frogs. A rustle in the trees gave her only a moment's warning before a young woman sprinted from the woods, toward the waiting pickup truck. Hunching in the seat, the teen broadcast anger and attitude even from a distance.

Troy came lumbering a few steps after, his broad shoulders carrying the weight of the world. Or rather the weight of one teen's defiance. Pretty much the same. And for tonight, at least, it could have been avoided if he hadn't been late in getting home from work. Guilt swamped her anew over taking up his evening with her embarrassing tumble.

He paused at the picket fence, his face somber even in the early dark. "Hey, I'm sorry to have left you hanging there. I needed to catch up with my daughter before she made a break for it."

She recalled his words in the truck about being at his wits end and wished she could help.

"I'm absolutely okay," Zelda rushed to assure him. "My sisters had a change of plans and are here to take care of me."

"Well, then, I need to get her home before she makes another break for it." He pushed away from the fence with a weary sigh. "I'm going to have to put a tracker on that kid—or take her to work with me."

She felt for him. And for his daughter, too.

Then inspiration struck with the perfect solution for how to sustain her workload and clear the feeling of debt to Troy.

"Troy?" she called out. "I'm in need of a dog washer to help at the grooming salon. I'd like to hire Harper."

Chapter Four

Troy wondered if his frustration with his daughter could have muddled his hearing. Surely he'd misunderstood Zelda. She couldn't possibly be asking for his daughter to come work at the grooming salon.

Pushing through the gate of the picket fence, he walked to the bottom of the steps, confident his daughter was secured in the truck. For now. "Zelda, what did you say?"

She cradled her scruffy little dog in her lap, her injured foot propped as she threaded her fingers through the yellow-white fur. "I want to hire Harper to be my dog washer at the grooming salon. I will spend less time on my feet and be able to focus on trims instead."

Boot on the bottom step, he scratched the back of his neck and recalled what a tough day she'd already had. "That's generous of you to offer, but are you sure you want to spend all day with a moody teen?"

He understood the way keeping up with his daughter could exhaust a person, but how could Zelda possibly know what that would be like? Although, as his gaze flicked toward the lit-up cabin behind her with shadows moving around inside, he remembered she had sisters. Maybe she understood better than he realized.

"I want to repay you for your help tonight." The porch light streamed down on her lovely face. "This way you won't have to worry about her wandering off and she can do her homework while I'm grooming."

Her proposition sounded like the answer to prayer—and a massive imposition. He crossed his arms and his boot slid slightly on the worn but sturdy wood. "That's a lot for me to ask of you. Harper could help for free."

"I don't want her to hate me, too—" Gasping, she stopped short, a blush rising on her cheeks. "Not that I'm saying she hates you."

The weight of her words only confirmed his own sense of failure when it came to reaching his daughter. He knew Harper was unhappy. With good reason, considering the raw deal she'd been given in the family department. Maybe being around Zelda would be good for her.

With a deep nod, he uncrossed his arms. "At the moment, she does." He hung his head and drew in a ragged sigh before meeting her gaze again. "I, uh, are you sure you can afford such an offer? I know Hollie and Jacob would understand if you need to cut back hours. And if not, I would be willing to pay her wages, just don't tell her it's from me."

Zelda was already shaking her head.

"I'm not cutting back, because I want this job to become a permanent one, which means making the best impression possible. As for the money, thank you for the offer, but I have a roof over my head and unlimited food from the lodge. My other bills are minor." She adjusted the pink bow on top of her pup's ears. Her delicate face set with determination—a glint in her eyes. "You don't have to decide now. In fact, you probably shouldn't answer before talking to Harper about it."

He glanced back at the truck, where his daughter was texting away with both thumbs, face lit from the screen of her phone, no doubt plotting her next escape. "I would be a fool to turn down your offer. I'm sure she would far rather hang with you and the dogs than spend the day with me. I'll discuss it with her, then reach back out to you tomorrow to talk more. If that's alright?"

"Perfect," she said with a smile that lit the night.

Clearing his throat, he leaned against the fat post framing the cabin porch. "How's your ankle feeling?"

He regretted not being able to help her into the house.

"Numb." Grinning, she gestured toward the humidity-soaked ice pack. "My sisters are both here now. They're bringing out our supper as we speak."

The cabin door creaked open with Isobel backing out carrying a tray laden with food.

Troy tipped his hat, easing away. "I'll leave you to it, then."

Pivoting on his bootheel, he jogged back to his pickup, the drive to his cabin carried out in total silence. Now wasn't the time to bring up anything. Best to wait until they were inside.

He barely had the truck in Park before Harper snatched her backpack off the floorboards and set a land-speed record running up the porch stairs. Sighing, he grabbed the to-go bag of dinners and started toward the cabin.

Much of the Top Dog Dude Ranch focused on dog-themed decor, but this cabin had more of an equine vibe that he appreciated. The soaring ceilings sported rafters with three vintage Western show saddles—each embroidered with thick, golden thread. Inside doors were all the sliding barn type. He couldn't have asked for a better place. If only he could get his daughter on board with the new start he was trying to give them both, as a family.

Harper stomped across the cabin and threw her backpack on the overstuffed brown sofa. "My life is ruined."

Closing and locking the front door behind him, he looked at his daughter, who had drawn her hair back into a messy bun, arms firmly crossed over her chest. His footsteps echoed on the wooden floors and off the vaulted ceilings up to Harper's bedroom loft.

He set the brown to-go bags down on the tall kitchenette table, careful not to knock over the horseshoe-shaped salt and pepper shakers. "I seriously doubt that."

"I have *no* social life." Harper skulked into the kitchen and yanked open the refrigerator to grab a soda. "*No* friends after tonight. And it's all your fault for dragging me off to this middle-of-nowhere, armpit of a place."

Teenage rage radiated off Harper's small frame as she moved back out of the kitchen close to the table.

An exhale that rivaled winter wind flared her nostrils as she fidgeted with the soda can.

"You're living in a resort." Troy passed her a napkin. "There are plenty of kids your age who would think you're living in a vacation."

"A vacation without a Starbucks," she wailed as she flounced out of the room, climbed the ladder to the loft and wrenched her sliding door closed so hard it rattled dully in the aftermath.

The napkin fluttered downward. He snagged it in midair as he stood at the bottom of the ladder.

He resisted the urge to demand she come back down right this minute, but given how his temper was still simmering, he opted to give them both some cool-down time.

Crinkling back the brown paper bag, he unloaded two to-go boxes before placing the meal he'd originally picked up for Zelda in the stainless steel refrigerator. Closing the fridge door, he turned to the open shelving on the kitchen wall and selected two ceramic blue dinner plates, along with utensils.

How did other parents manage to cook and feed their kid at the end of a long workday?

After he set the table, taking his time in order to calm down, he called, "Hey, kiddo, dinner's ready."

She still didn't answer.

He had only one reliable tool in his parenting toolbox, and as much as he hated to use it, he was at his wits end. "Harper, I am your father and we need to talk. You can come out and speak or I'm going to have to turn off your cell phone."

Silence echoed for a solid thirty seconds before the lock sounded on her door and she climbed down the ladder from the loft. She sat at the dinette table and slammed down her soda, a dribble sloshing over the side of the can.

Gathering his thoughts, he wadded up the napkin before joining her at the table. "Harper, I realize you don't want to be here, but I'm responsible for your safety."

"Dad," she sighed in exasperation, pushing her cowboy corn around the plate, "we never left the ranch and we were only gonna talk…maybe kiss, but nothing more."

He wasn't going to debate that with her. Not tonight when they were both so tense.

Spearing pulled pork on his fork, he quirked an eyebrow at his daughter. "Regardless, you broke the rule about not wandering off without letting me know where you're going. So I'm going to give you two choices of how you want to spend your time until I can trust you alone again. First option, you can come to work with me—and trust me when I say that Wynn will not be in the same barn."

Her speedy squawk of denial would have made him laugh if he wasn't so heartbroken. What had happened to his little girl who used to beg to hang around the stables and go horseback riding with him?

No one prepared you for the kick in gut of the feeling when your kid no longer wants to spend time with you. "Harper, the second choice—you can take a summer job with Zelda Dalton at the grooming salon. She will pay you to wash dogs. The choice is yours, but those are the only two options for the next month. That is a consequence of your actions tonight."

Taking a bite of the corn bread, he waited for her to digest his offer.

Harper turned her can around and around, not meeting his eyes. But he could see the wheels churning all the same.

"Fine," she said through gritted teeth. "I'll wash the dogs."

Before he could respond, she climbed the ladder again, this time closing the door softly. He would take that as a win. Although he'd never had a win tire him out this much.

His cell phone chimed with an incoming text—a welcome distraction from the stifling air between himself and Harper. He tugged his phone from his pocket and found...

Zelda's name.

A jolt of surprise, mixed with excitement, shot through him. They'd exchanged numbers at the doctor's clinic so she could reach him if need be while he picked up the food that she'd never gotten to share.

He thumbed open the message.

Is everything okay with your daughter?

He glanced up to the loft, then down at the partially finished soda resting in the slosh puddle alongside the uneaten meals. Sighing, he pushed to his feet, grabbed his plate and shouldered through the porch door. He dropped onto the sturdy log rocker. Rather than text a response, he tapped Call before he could second-guess himself. After the crummy exchange with Harper, he needed a distraction.

A distraction?

He had to admit that his attraction to Zelda Dalton was proving to be far more than a simple *distraction*.

She answered the call. "Well, hello. Did you break your texting fingers?"

Grinning, he swirled water in his cup. "This was quicker than typing out a response. Are you free to talk?"

"My sisters just left," she said, her voice maybe a little breathless as an owl hooted in the distance. "I'm sitting on my porch with my foot up while my dog runs around inside the fence."

"Sorry I didn't get to give you the dinner box." He looked past the line of trees, toward the nearby trio of cabins where she and her sisters lived. If he tilted his head at the right angle, he could just barely make out her shadowy silhouette on a rocker, her foot propped up on the railing. "Would you like me to walk it over? I won't stay. I need to get back home to keep watch over my wayward teen."

"Thanks for the offer. My sisters fed me well and pampered me before they left," she answered. "You can just enjoy the boxed dinner as seconds."

"Thirds, actually, since Harper refused to do more than pick at hers." He thought about their argument, feeling more unsettled than ever. Soft music streamed down from her loft. "She's locked herself in her bedroom."

He scooped fluffy mashed potatoes onto his fork, the gravy oozing onto his plate.

"I'm so sorry," she said, with genuine sympathy. "Did you find out why Harper and Wynn were out?"

"She swears they were just going to walk and make out, nothing more. But how can I trust her?" Frustration knotted tighter as he thought of the blanket tucked under her arm as she headed off with that boy. "Forget I said any of that. I didn't mean to unload on you. We barely know each other."

In part because he'd been doing his best to avoid her—and the attraction. He'd made it clear to her right after they met that he was focused on his kid.

"No need to apologize," she assured him. "It must be tough keeping up with a teenager. It's not like you can lock her in a closet."

"Aside from that being morally wrong and illegal," he said, glancing over his shoulder into the cabin, "Harper would pick the lock."

Her chuckle warmed him through the phone lines, echoing in the night breeze. "Well, I can appreciate that skill set after the day that I had getting locked in at the grooming salon. Have you given any further thought to my job offer?"

"If you're absolutely sure, we gratefully accept." Even as he agreed, his conscience still pinched him, hard. For his daughter, he would have to get over it, though. "I spoke to Harper about it and she made it clear she would prefer to spend the day washing dogs than hanging out with me."

"I'm glad to have her help," she said graciously.

Zelda really was a thoughtful person, underneath the sometimes prickly exterior. He wondered what had brought that about.

"I'll drive my daughter, of course." He paused, wiping his mouth with his napkin. "And since I'm heading that way, I am happy to pick you up, as well. It'll make things easier for you while you let that sprain heal."

"Oh," she gasped in surprise, "uh, thank you. I'll see you around seven o'clock?"

"Bright and early." He paused, holding on to the connection a moment beyond wise. A moment that hinted at wanting...more. Reckless. Especially given how much time they would be spending together over the next few weeks. "Good night, Zelda."

And as he disconnected the call with her farewell echoing in his memory, he couldn't deny that for the first time in a long time, he was looking forward to tomorrow.

The next morning, Zelda sat on the edge of the forest green sofa, propping her foot on the coffee table to rewrap it before Troy came by to pick her up. She wasn't sure how they'd gone from avoiding each other to starting and finishing each day together, but she couldn't deny the excitement in the pit of her belly over seeing him soon.

If only she wasn't too exhausted to enjoy the sensation. Her aching ankle had kept her up most of the night. Then showering had been a challenge—and her cabin didn't have a tub so she'd been stuck wrapping her foot in a garbage bag. She knew she could have reached out to Isobel since their cabin had wheelchair-accessible facilities for little Lottie.

Except pride got the better of her, and she didn't want to disrupt her niece's routine. Lottie's health was in such a precarious state as they searched for a new kidney donor match, since their only possible match thus far had become too sick to donate. As if the six-year-old didn't already have enough challenges after being born with spina bifida.

Zelda felt small for whining over a sore ankle. So she'd taken a barstool into the shower stall. It wasn't even seven o'clock in the morning and she was already worn out.

Again, sympathy for her niece bit her on the conscience. Hard. This time in Moonlight Ridge was supposed to be about expanding the donor search. The child's needs were top-priority important. The whole reason she'd chosen this place for her escape from her ex.

But no question, Troy Shaw had proved to be a big distraction from the very first day she'd arrived—another embarrassing encounter she cringed in remembering…

Finally, finally she'd arrived at her little summer cottage. Zelda scooped up Maisey from the front seat of her little VW bug and flung open the door.

A light rumble vibrated the earth under her feet. Surely, they didn't have earthquakes here.

Wouldn't that be just her luck?

Then the sound of horse hooves echoed, growing closer, giving her a moment's warning before a palomino nosed through the forest, ridden by a cowboy about fifty feet away. At least she assumed he was a cowboy. A Stetson was tipped low over his eyes, shading his face from view.

A vacationer?

Or an employee?

Either way, her pastoral paradise had been invaded.

She had no time for anyone except her family and her animal clients. So unless the cowboy had a shaggy pooch, their paths would not be crossing.

Cradling her Maltese mix, she made fast tracks for her cabin, trotting up the steps and stopping at the door to punch in the security code from the confirmation email. She tapped the lock once.

Twice.

A third time.

The lock blared red repeatedly.

She slumped back against the porch post. Maisey swiveled her head from Zelda to the door, then back again. "I know. I'm trying."

No doubt she'd jammed up the whole thing, like using a password too many times, then navigating a contorted process of verifying identity.

"Do you need some help?"

A voice rumbled over her senses, vibrating the air around her as tangibly as those hoofbeats had shaken the earth. Sighing, she closed her eyes for a moment before turning to the witness to her embarrassment.

Yep.

The tall, dark and cocky cowboy.

She hated the defensiveness—worse yet, the insecurity—that seared through her until her ears rung. She hated the self-doubt, a reminder that her ex still had a hold over her, even from a distance. It wasn't this stranger's fault she couldn't work the stupid door lock.

But she also wasn't going to give the code to a stranger. Which meant she would have to get back into her car and go to the main lodge for assistance.

She braced her shoulders and forced a smile. "Thanks for the offer, but we're okay. Right, Maisey?"

He stared at her for so long she thought for a moment that he would press the point.

Then he tipped his Stetson and clicked his horse into motion. "Have a nice day, ma'am."

As she cradled her dog to her chest and ran to the safety of her little Beetle, she couldn't escape the truth racing after her. She wasn't okay. Not at all...

A knock on the door shook Zelda from her thoughts and had her scrambling to grab her crutches. She wasn't anywhere near ready for work and she cringed inside to think of how her stress about that traced back to old interactions with her ex. Even now, she could almost feel his irritation at moments like this.

Her ex had always become so angry when she lost track of time, calling her an inconsiderate daydreamer. She checked her watch and found—yes, she should have had at least another half hour to finish dressing, so she wasn't at fault. At least she had her clothes on, if not her shoes. She would have to braid her wet hair on the ride over.

"Maisey, girl," Zelda said as she tucked the crutches under her arms. "I need you to move out of the way. I can't afford another tumble anytime soon."

Maisey dropped into a pretty sit, tilting her head to the side. She truly was the best furry buddy. Zelda would have been totally lost without her during that dark last year with her ex.

Juggling the crutches, she managed to pluck a treat out of the container on the end table before hobbling to the door. She took a deep breath to still her hammering heart and tugged open the door.

Only to deflate.

Neve waited on her stoop, holding a basket with juice bottles and a bakery bag. "Good morning, sister dear. I'm here to keep you company—or drive you back to the doctor. I brought blackberry muffins and orange juice."

"That's so thoughtful, but I'm heading into work in about a half hour." Zelda wasn't used to having anyone tend to her, but she was really grateful to feel safe in her own home after the minute of old tension that had streaked through her at the thoughts of her ex-boyfriend. She eyed the basket of muffins appreciatively, her mouth watering. "Although I wouldn't mind taking one of those to go."

"Well, then, a half hour to spare? You have time to

eat breakfast—or watch me while I eat. You can enjoy the leftover ones later." Neve strode past into the small cabin, her hiking boots thudding ever so softly on the paw-patterned rug. Her yoga pants, tank top and fanny pack broadcast her hiking plans. "Are you sure a full day on your feet is wise?"

Zelda rested the crutches against the sofa, then hopped past a massive carved dog on her way over to the table. "I have a helper for the dog-washing portion so I can focus on the trims. If it gets to be too much, I'll speak up."

"I would hope so." Neve pulled out a couple of plump muffins and placed each one on a napkin. She waved a hand over them, wafting the sweet berry scent through the room. "Come on, sit for a moment. Have a bite to eat while they're still warm. It'll give you time to ice your ankle again. Or maybe you'll let me braid your hair."

The mention of braiding her hair sparked older, happy memories.

Still, Zelda hesitated. She hated being needy, vulnerable, but the determined look on Neve's face spoke volumes. Besides, her stomach was grumbling. "Okay, thank you." She sat at the table and propped her foot on another chair. "I appreciate all you're doing for me. I can finish my hair later. I don't want to keep you from your work."

"My schedule is flexible. Remember? I'm on sabbatical for my research project." Neve foraged through the kitchenette drawers and pulled out a Ziploc bag, then moved to the ice maker. "I have time to share this morning before my bird-watching."

Zelda knew Neve was downplaying the complexity of her work. While they all three valued education, Neve had always been the truest bookworm of the sisters. More often than not, she could be found in the forest with a couple of novels. Neve enjoyed her solitude.

Which made Zelda feel all the more guilty for keeping her from her plans. And even guiltier for not asking more about her sister's scientific undertaking— something to do with bird wildlife. "Are you still on track to finish your research? Is there something I can do to help?"

Although as soon as she said that, a sense of helplessness washed over her at how little she could do to help anyone. Maybe that was a part of why giving Harper an outlet at the grooming felt so right.

"I have until after the Christmas break before I return to the classroom." She rested the ice bag on Zelda's ankle, then pulled out two bottles of orange juice from the bag. "After we finish breakfast, I can drive you to the salon."

"Oh, uh, I already have a ride." Zelda peeled the paper away from her muffin with undue concentration. "Since Harper is my new dog washer, Troy will be picking me up—the practical solution."

"Really? The same 'Troy' who took you to see Doc Barnett, then waited around to bring you home?" A smirk played with Neve's mouth. "Are you sure your lingering was all about practicality?"

Zelda bit off half the muffin to keep from answering, partly because she didn't want to stoke any rumors.

And also because she didn't have an answer for herself, either.

Chapter Five

Troy shifted the truck into Park outside Zelda's cabin and twisted in his seat toward his daughter where she slouched in back. Harper hadn't spoken much today, and he'd been trying to give her some space.

But the time had come to remind her of what was at stake with this job. "Harper, no slacking off today. Don't forget that you're a paid employee. If Zelda fires you, then you'll have to come to work with me." His fingers drummed against the leather of his steering wheel before narrowing his eyes. *"For free."*

"Got it," she said without meeting his gaze, then slid from the pickup, feet thudding. Hands tucked in her jeans' back pockets, she strode up the walkway and greeted Zelda.

Manners?

Well, wonders never ceased. He'd planned to walk to that front door himself, but then he couldn't deny himself this glimpse of Harper that he hadn't seen in a while.

He knew his daughter had been taught manners, he just hadn't seen much evidence of late. Maybe this would work out even better than he'd planned.

Just as fast, he pushed down the optimistic thought. Expectation management was key when it came to his teen. He needed to keep his hopes in check.

Troy slid from the truck and jogged up the front walkway where Zelda was seated, braiding her hair with her dog on her lap. His eyes were drawn like magnets to the smooth movements of her fingers working a silver band at the end of her braid.

"Good morning, Troy," Zelda called in a sunny voice. "And Harper, too. Perfect timing."

His daughter scuffed her pink gym shoe on the paver stone. Silently. Her manners must have evaporated.

Zelda tapped the wicker basket beside her. "I have blackberry muffins, in case anyone's hungry. Mornings are always so hectic."

Harper cleared her throat. "What should I carry for you?"

Zelda lifted her dog from her lap and set her on the porch. A wide, thoughtful grin pushed dimples into her cheeks. "You know what I need most? I want to bring my dog, Maisey, to work. If you could hold her in the truck and settle her at the salon, that would be a tremendous help."

"Sure." Harper smiled, a first in a long time.

At least around him.

He breathed a sigh of relief that for the first time in months, his daughter looked...not angry. He wouldn't go so far as to say she appeared happy. But the hurt and anger that she wore like a defensive cloak had softened enough that he could see glimmers of his child from years past.

In the quirk of her lips, he could see the five-year-old kid who'd asked to be picked up, currycomb in hand. She'd been so eager back then to learn how to care for horses. Once, she'd begged to learn barrel racing and Troy's heart swelled with pride at her interest—and her knack for the sport.

As Maisey trotted down the steps, the teen knelt, extending a hand for the little Maltese mix to sniff. "She's cute."

"She likes you." Zelda nodded in approval as she stood and tucked her crutches into place. "That's a good sign for our working relationship."

Troy grabbed Zelda's elbow instinctively to steady her. Her braid brushed his arm and he willed down the urge to brush it against his face to test the texture, to breathe in the scent.

Instead, once he'd made sure she was steady on her crutches, he stepped back, determined to keep his distance and control for his daughter's sake. He couldn't risk upending the apple cart, especially not now, with the memory of his daughter's smile still fresh.

Pointing to his truck, he channeled the inner calm he used for particularly difficult rodeo stunts. "Alright, ladies, ready to load up for work?"

Zelda had to admit, she was enjoying having company in the grooming salon. While yes, she adored the dogs that she tended, having a human voice chime in made the time pass. She'd grown too accustomed to silence.

Yet another thing she intended to change in her life. No more isolation, even if reentering the world still stirred butterflies in her stomach. Focusing on work helped, though.

Parked at the grooming table, Zelda had lowered the height so she could sit with her foot elevated. The door between the salon and reception hall had been removed and a doggy gate installed. A refreshing mountain breeze swept through so much cooler than summers in Atlanta.

Maisey slept in a dog bed under the grooming table. These days she snoozed more and more, her age beginning to show. All the more reason Zelda had been glad to bring her dog along and keep an eye on her.

Luckily, today's appointments were all small breed. She swept her thinning sheers through the fur of a Pomeranian mix with the cutest face and the biggest of attitudes. His family had gone swimming in the hot springs. Her next client waited in a kennel, a graying Pekingese. Her "mama and daddy" wanted her gussied up for the big cookout at the ranch's glamping campground full of restored vintage RVs.

The day promised a lighter schedule, for sure, but still one she couldn't have managed today without Harper's help. "I'm thankful you agreed to come work with me."

Harper stood at the industrial steel sink, wearing a waterproof smock and washing the ranch owner's Scottish terrier—Scottie. Droplets splashed on her face, dampening her feathered bangs. "It's better than sitting around the cabin all day."

"The quiet can get old pretty fast." Zelda trimmed along the edges of the Pomeranian's ears.

"I have my phone." Chewing her bottom lip nervously, Harper moved the sprayer along Scottie's sudsy body, avoiding his eyes and nose. The scent of vanilla filled the air as the bubbles swirled down the drain. Scottie huffed, shaking water droplets everywhere. A small, tenuous smile tugged at the teen as she scratched between his ears. "I call my friends back home when I'm not busy with mountains of homework."

Poor kid. It didn't sound like much of a summer. But Zelda understood Troy's concern. "If you need to take a break after you finish with Scottie, we could have lunch or I can help you with that homework."

For a moment, Zelda thought the teen would agree to one or the other of her offers. There'd been no mistaking the wistful look in Harper's eyes.

But as fast as it appeared, it faded, hidden behind a disdainful mask. "Nah," Harper said. "I can manage. And the sooner I finish washing dogs, the sooner we can be done for the day."

"Okay, then." Zelda lifted the clippers, giving them a little shake. "Let's power on."

The chimes on the front door announced a new arrival even though there wasn't another client due for an hour. Zelda leaned to check...

And found her sister and niece coming through the front door. Isobel pushed Lottie's wheelchair, while the little girl's service dog trotted alongside.

"Yoo-hoo," Isobel called.

"Hi, Auntie Zelda, Cocoa needs a bath." Lottie scrunched up her nose, looking too adorable with her twin braids sporting paw-print ribbons.

Isobel eyed the full kennel, washtub and grooming table. "If you have time today?"

"Come on in," Zelda answered, wiping her palm on her smock. "Thanks to my new helper here, we absolutely can give Cocoa a deluxe spa treatment."

Harper waved a sudsy hand, the yellow rubber glove covered in bubbles.

"Awesome," Isobel said just as her cell phone started ringing. She smiled her apology and stepped into the reception area, her voice low and professional.

"Yay!" Lottie cheered, her fists in the air, before wheeling closer to Zelda for a heart-melting hug. "Cocoa got really stinky rolling around in the mud last night. She couldn't sleep on my bed with me, and that made me super sad."

Zelda had seen firsthand how Cocoa pressed her body just so against Lottie's legs at night to help ease neuropathy pain. Even now, the dog pressed her head against Lottie's thigh.

"Well, we can take care of that smelly-pup problem and have her smelling like vanilla cookies." Zelda set aside her scissors and unhooked the now pristine Pom mix.

She scooted her rolly chair over to a small kennel and placed the Pom inside, before turning a fan on low. The fluffy scrap gave an exhausted sigh and curled up to sleep on the fresh towel inside the pen.

Zelda secured the latch and turned to Lottie. "Do you want to stay here with her or do you have plans for the afternoon?"

"When Mommy finishes her phone call, we're going to Mr. Troy's riding camp. That's my favorite pack-tivity." Lottie smiled at Harper, pointing toward her purple cowboy boots. "I'll tell your daddy you said howdy."

Harper pulled a decent attempt at a smile, still rinsing suds off Scottie. "Thanks, kid. I'm sure you'll have a great time."

Lottie leaned forward conspiratorially. "Harper, you should keep your cell phone put away. Aunt Zelda had to get a new one 'cause one of these dogs dropped her old one in a bucket of water."

"That's what I hear. Thanks for the reminder, though." Grinning, Harper patted her back pocket over the outline of her phone.

No matter how many times Zelda was reminded of the water bucket story, it never made her feel any less silly.

Lottie's hand fell to rest on her chocolate Labrador's head. "Cocoa would have helped Aunt Zelda. She wouldn't have made things tougher like that bad puppy. I wish I could let Cocoa help my aunt. Except I'm not supposed to let Cocoa listen to anybody except me or my mom."

The generosity of the thought made Zelda's heart squeeze. "And I wouldn't want to keep Cocoa from being there for you. Thank you for offering, though. That was very kind of you."

Lottie tapped her chin, her face lighting with inspiration. "Maybe I can give you some tips to get around better."

Zelda reached to pat Lottie's elbow. "That would be lovely. Thank you, sweetie. You're the best niece ever."

Footsteps sounded in the reception area an instant before Isobel poked her head back in the room as she tucked her cell phone into her pocket. "Are we all set for Cocoa?"

"Absolutely." Zelda gestured toward an extra-large crate with a fluffy bed inside. "Cocoa can stay as long as you need. We've got a comfy kennel for her to nap in while she dries. Go enjoy yourself."

Isobel cued Cocoa into the kennel and rewarded her with a treat before clasping the handles of her daughter's wheelchair. "Thank you, sis. I'll keep you posted on the time."

After door chimes announced their departure, Harper grabbed a stack of paw-print towels and began to rub down Scottie. Her cheeks puffed with a sigh, her gaze soft. "I'm not sure if it's okay to ask, but what happened to Lottie? I heard she needs a kidney, but what's up with her wheelchair?"

"It's fine with me if you ask." Zelda scooted the wheeled stool over to Cocoa's kennel, opened the door and began trimming her nails. "Lottie was born with a birth defect called spina bifida. That means a part of her spine and the membranes around it didn't close fully. So there's nerve damage. Kidney function complications are common."

"That's rough." Harper's forehead furrowed in sympathy. "Can't her mom or you or Neve donate? I mean, I know that's a lot to ask of somebody else. But you're family."

"I would if I could, and so would Neve, but we're not a match." The grief of that haunted her, making her feel all the more useless. And no matter how much compassionate self-talk she deployed to try and remind herself that wasn't true, she still had trouble shaking the way her ex-boyfriend had destroyed her sense of self-worth.

Blowing a damp strand of hair from her forehead with a huff, Harper gently scooped Scottie up into her arms, leaving the pile of damp towels in the steel sink. "How does someone find out if they're a match?"

The sincere interest in the teen's eyes warmed Zelda's heart, assuring her there was a lot of good character inside Troy's daughter no matter what else she might be struggling with right now.

"The process starts with a blood test," Zelda said, then rushed to add. "But you're a minor."

Her face fell as she placed Scottie on the grooming table and attached the tether. Overhead, the sound of the fan buzzed, the only noise for a few thunderous heartbeats. "Maybe I can help in other ways."

"Of course you can, thank you, as long as your dad is okay with it." Smiling at Harper, Zelda rolled the chair back toward Scottie and propped her throbbing ankle on the chair again. The little terrier panted before stretching and yawning. "That's really thoughtful of you."

"It's better than being stuck in the cabin or following

my dad around all the time." Harper checked the latch on Cocoa's kennel, then the Pom's. Already, Harper seemed committed to doing a good job—to being useful. Her thoughtful care for the animals was obvious.

"Well, there's another donor drive coming up at the end of the summer junior rodeo. Hopefully, this will be the winning ticket. We had a possible donor located, but he got a horrible case of mono."

"That's rotten luck," Harper said, shaking her head. "What kind of tests do they need to find out if someone can be a donor?"

"Well, to start, blood tests for blood type, tissue matching, cross-matching, check for antibodies..." Zelda ticked off on her fingers. "I think I got that right. It's a whole new world to me and I'm still learning the ins and outs. The results take about a week."

"Wow, what can I do to help?"

Zelda smoothed a soothing hand along Scottie to gauge when the dog was calm enough for her to commence trimming. He licked her hand and settled. "We'll need people to man the sign-up table. And we may do a dog wash. That was really popular last time and we have had a whole bunch of new guests arrive at the ranch since then."

Casting a wary side-eye toward Zelda, Harper scooped up the towels from the wash sink and tossed them into the hamper. Her curtain bangs falling into her face, hiding the rise of a blush. "Maybe Wynn would like to pitch in, too."

Zelda paused trimming for a moment, weighing her reply, while outside children's laughter echoed. No doubt guests on their way to more pack-tivities. She inhaled the fresh mountain air and resumed clipping Scottie. "What do you think your father would say?"

Harper dropped to the floor beside Maisey's bed, petting the snoozing furball. Maisey's light raspy snores mixed with the sound of the fan, creating a soundscape of white noise. "He would say to lock me in the cellar until I'm a hundred and eighteen."

"I'm sure that's not true." The clicking of shears echoed between them.

"But..." Harper said carefully, "if *you* ask him about Wynn..."

Zelda shook her head fast, her braid whipping along her back as she set aside the clippers for a comb. "I'm not getting between you and your father."

"I thought you were one of the cool adults," she mumbled under her breath, stroking Maisey. Then winced, looking up fast. "Sorry. Please don't fire me."

"You're a hard worker. Keep on being a hard worker and we'll be fine." Zelda slid a comb through Scottie's silky fur, her chair squeaking as she shifted. "You can ask your father about the donor drive, and if he tells me it's okay, then I'll gratefully accept the help."

"Thank you." Harper sighed in relief before standing, dusting the fur clippings from her jeans before returning to the sink to scrub it down with sanitizer. The crisp scent filled the room as she poured the cleaner. Turning on the faucet, Harper set to work, her face tight.

"Harper?" she called, weighing her words carefully, hoping she wasn't overstepping. "Give your dad a chance. Okay? He's doing his best to keep you safe."

She just prayed Troy would understand that barring his daughter from seeing Wynn at all could lead to even more dangerous behavior. Because Zelda knew from her own experience that even the smartest of people didn't always make the wisest of choices when it came to romance.

Wynn Oakes hated that he'd blown it. Again.

Gloved hands gripping the wood rod of the red plastic muck fork, he couldn't fight off the sick feeling in his stomach. Landing this summer internship with his idol—Troy Shaw—had been a real dream come true. Wynn almost hadn't applied, figuring why bother, but his folks had encouraged him because they said it might look good on a college resume—and that he really, really needed the extra help. Apparently even they saw what a loser he was at everything else.

The space well-lit from skylights, he surveyed two stalls he still had left. This barn was smaller than the ranch's main barn, but still boasted eight stalls. Eight stalls for eight horses he'd been trusted to work with. The opportunity of a lifetime.

A heaviness sat on his chest as he entered the second-to-last stall, starting to sift the bedding. He'd never been good at anything until he discovered the rodeo world by chance, answering an advertisement to muck out a horse barn for extra money. It was the only part-time job he'd been able to find that started with an in-person interview. Everywhere else, he had to start with the online application, which just made him feel stupid.

He didn't feel dumb on the back of a horse, taking those barrels at a breakneck speed. The roar of the crowd was so much louder than the taunts in the classroom, he could almost forget them.

Almost.

Until times like this when Troy Shaw—a real rodeo king—looked at him like he was as useless as gum on a bootheel.

"Sir?" Wynn set aside the muck fork and warily approached Troy at the crossties with one of the horses—a dark bay named Dandelion. "I want to apologize for last night. I shouldn't have asked your daughter out without your permission."

"Agreed," Troy growled out in a tone that left little hope for forgiveness. He grabbed a currycomb and started working up dirt, moving down Dandelion's body from shoulder to hindquarter without looking away.

"So I'm asking now." Wynn gave Dandelion a pat on the neck, scavenging for courage. The horse nickered in response, a sign he took as gentle encouragement. He'd been in such disbelief that Harper had noticed him, he'd been afraid to waste even an instant waiting. "I would like to take your daughter out on a date. A proper date."

Wynn did his best to stand tall, square his shoulders, and readied himself to meet his hero's gaze. A horse whinnied at the other end of barn, the sound slicing through the chatter of guests who were trying on different helmets with another ranch hand for an upcoming ride.

Troy pivoted slowly, knuckling the brim of his Stetson up, his eyes narrowing to lasers. "Son, you need to learn the art of timing. *In* and *out* of the saddle. This is not the right time for that question."

Wynn winced, his stomach sinking like during his last rodeo competition where he'd misjudged the distance and sent his horse crashing into the last barrel. "You're still mad."

Sighing, Wynn dragged the toe of his boot through the dusty earth. He didn't know when he would have another chance like this. Before long, he would be starting his senior year. If he even managed to pass. Which was doubtful.

"I'm frustrated that my daughter was put in an unsafe situation." His voice tight, Troy picked up a hard brush, beginning to firmly brush off the loose dirt and hair. For a moment, the only sound was the soft whisk of the brush against the horse. Wynn looked on, hands tucking into his jean pocket. Troy dropped the hard brush into the grooming box, anger feathering through his brows. He grabbed a hoof pick. "Wandering around at night like that is dangerous. I already suspected I couldn't trust her. But now I can't trust you, either, and that's a big disappointment, personally and professionally."

The weight of Troy's disapproval hit Wynn again, along with echoes of his classmates' voices listing his faults. His school papers affirming his failures and worthlessness. His heart beat too hard and fast.

And if he'd cost himself this internship as well as any chance with Harper...?

Even the possibility made him feel like throwing up. "So you're saying there's no chance I can take her out? Ever?"

"Wynn?" Troy said low, but firm. "Remember. Timing."

"Right. Gotcha." He returned to his un-mucked stall and began working furiously.

Because even though he threw around phrases like "gotcha," he would have appreciated a better explanation of what Troy meant. What was the right time to ask for permission? After Harper graduated? Next week?

When Troy was in a good mood?

As Wynn filled the wheelbarrow and freshened the stall with new bedding, he lost himself in the work, trying hard to show he was worth something. Every lift of the muck fork came with beads of sweat between his shoulder blades, even with the industrial fan blowing the mountain air from one side of the stable to the other.

He wasn't sure how to make things right. He wasn't sure how to explain that he didn't know all the manners and rules. No one had taught him at home. He'd tried to soak up as much as he could at school, but learning—especially reading—was already so hard, sometimes he didn't have the brain space for anything more.

Moving to the next stall, he was proud of creating a clean environment for the horses he loved. This much, he could control. But frustration still gnawed on him about the rest of his life until his stomach was in knots as he filled the wheelbarrow to the brim.

Setting aside the muck fork, he grasped the two wooden levers of the wheelbarrow. Straining against the weight, he began to move toward the compost pit while disappointment snaked through him. He hated falling into a pity party, but sometimes his life sucked so much, he wasn't sure how to keep putting one foot in front of the other.

His senior year loomed large and depressing, full of all the ways he would disappoint his parents. Again. He wanted to drop out and just hit the rodeo circuit for real, but his folks kept reminding him how one injury in the ring could leave him with no means of support.

Sometimes he wondered if getting hurt would be such a bad thing. He could be homeschooled online, away from people laughing at him. And it wasn't like anyone would notice if he lost a few IQ points.

"Hey, Wynn?" Troy's voice cut through his dark cloud.

"Yes, sir?" Wary, he paused by Dandelion, the mare's tail swishing away flies.

"I can't control where you choose to sit at mealtime, but if you happen to be in the chow hall at the same time we are, I won't say no if you decide to sit with us."

Wynn stood straighter, barely able to believe his ears, his luck. "Thank you, sir."

Troy simply nodded, his Stetson covering his eyes, before walking forward with Dandelion to a waiting guest.

And in that moment, an instant Wynn didn't take for granted, he didn't want to ride off into the mountains until he disappeared.

Chapter Six

By the end of the workday, Troy still couldn't figure out how he'd gone from putting Wynn in his place, to extending an open invitation to dinner. Something about the kid, a sadness and insecurity radiating off him, caught Troy by surprise. So far, though, he hadn't seen the boy since then and they'd already finished eating.

Of course, he could have avoided the possibility of running into each other altogether by taking Harper straight home for a supper that didn't involve the chow hall. He'd been sincere enough in his invitation to the kid, but it wouldn't hurt to build in an extra day for everyone to cool off a bit more.

Instead, Troy found himself on a checkered picnic blanket with Zelda, his daughter and little Maisey. To be fair, the thought of hanging out in the small cabin with his sulking daughter hadn't sounded appealing. At all. Besides, she'd been smiling when he stopped by the grooming salon to pick them up after work.

And yes, he'd wanted to extend that joy for as long as possible, the gathering reminding him of the week

Zelda had arrived, her presence encompassing even the simplest of gatherings such as a bonfire gathering...

Tossing his paper plate into the fire, Troy stood to pluck up a skewer for himself only to find his seat taken and nowhere left except next to Zelda. "Glad everything worked out for you, with the lock and all. A frustrating start to your vacation, no doubt."

She looked up with startled eyes as she unwrapped a mini chocolate bar. "Thank you."

Not much of a talker, was she? He stabbed two marshmallows on the spike and held it over the fire, just above the flame. "I realized after the fact that you must have worried about me being privy to your cabin code." He regretted not handling the introduction better. He wasn't a green kid by any means, but when he'd seen her standing there on her porch, his brain cells seemed to have taken a hike for the hills. "I should have identified myself as an employee."

She quirked her eyebrow, smashing her s'more together. "That would have been helpful. Not that I would have taken you at your word, though. Anyone in a cowboy hat can claim to work here."

"True enough." Smart woman, who also had a deeply wary look darkening her pretty blue eyes, making the reflected flames all the brighter. "You're not much of a trusting soul."

"And you're making assumptions. Such as assuming I'm on vacation. I work at the ranch, too." She took a bite of the graham cracker treat with a self-satisfied smirk.

Seriously? Not a guest? But an employee, too, and all that entailed for being at the same functions for his entire summer? So much for only needing to hold strong for a week or two. Sure, he thrived on a challenge in the rodeo ring, but the stakes here were too high. His daughter was already acting out to the point of being picked up by the police for truancy last spring. He needed to do whatever it took to give her the stability she needed.

"I stand corrected, ma'am. I guess that means I'll be seeing you around the ranch." He pulled his skewer away from the flame, wishing it could be that simple to distance himself from the smoking-hot temptation of this woman...

Now, as he dined with Zelda on a picnic blanket—with his daughter as well—Troy wasn't any closer to figuring out how to navigate even a simple gathering with her.

The mini "town square" was alive with guests and staff, name tags identifying the employees. People mixed with each other, conversations flowing like a Tennessee river winding through surrounding mountains. Down-to-earth, utterly peaceful, and blessedly lacking in the flicker and glare of digital technology. A serenity he needed with his life in such turmoil.

The scent of seasoned, grilled meat wafted from a vintage covered wagon—a chuck wagon, according to the lettering along the canvas—perched off to one side. Tables with red-checkered tablecloths were filled with a buffet of covered dishes where the latest round of diners lined up. The massive chalkboard menu noted s'mores for dessert at the bonfire.

A sound system crackling to life drew his attention to the dais where the couple who owned the ranch—his bosses—waved their matching ebony Stetsons at the crowd. Jacob O'Brien gripped the microphone. "Welcome to Moonlight Ridge, Tennessee, home of the Top Dog Dude Ranch and the magical Sulis Cave."

Cheers and whoops lifted from the crowd. Flames licked up toward the sky where stars were just beginning to wink down. The ranch's welcome dinner took place once a week outside the main lodge, with everyone dressed up in Western gear. Not some sleek, wealthy-dude-ranch sort of clothing. But the broken-in kind. This place sported an earthy, natural vibe that called to the authentic cowboy within him. He hoped to create something similar with his training center…

"I'm your host, Jacob, and this lovely lady…" He gestured to the woman at his side, her jeans and green plaid shirt matching his as his smile widened. "This beautiful lady is my wife, Hollie, and also the magnificent chef at our Bone Appetit Café. And those four rascals over there are our children, getting ready for the play later this evening about the legend of Sulis Cave."

Jacob waved toward three boys and a little girl with glasses, all wearing identical Top Dog Dude Ranch T-shirts. "When Hollie and I founded the Top Dog Dude Ranch, we planned for it to be more than a vacation spot. We wanted to create a haven, a place of refuge with tools available to enhance your life. It's our hope that through our enrichment 'pack-tivities,' you carry a piece of the Top Dog experience with you when you return home."

Moving closer to her husband, Hollie swept back her dark ponytail. "If you came here with burdens on your heart, we hope that your time here will do more than refresh you. But that you'll also find peace."

Troy was all in on that. He and his daughter would need a boatload of those pack-tivities.

Jacob slung an arm around his wife's shoulders as he continued, "And if you're wondering where to start, during breakfast tomorrow there will be a newcomers' session to acquaint you with the many options available at our ranch. Our staff will be there sharing about their specialties, including our expanded spa features and our newly added whitewater rafting opportunities."

Hollie clapped her hands together as an evening mountain breeze swept through. "If you're an early riser, you may want to stop by our baby goat yoga class by the river. Now, without further ado, time to help yourself to seconds of our barbecue buffet and enjoy music from our very own Raise the Woof band."

Near the bonfire, a live band leaped onto a flatbed wagon with guitars, a banjo and a fiddle. The drummer took his place on a bale of hay, clicking his drumsticks together to set the beat before a country tune filled the early night air. Troy's toe twitched to the beat and he itched to dig up his harmonica and join in. There hadn't been much time for hobbies or R & R lately.

Zelda's head bobbed with the music, her dark braid swaying against her left shoulder as she kept time with the beat of the drums.

Troy tipped his head toward her. "You'll be dancing again before you know it."

She went still, looking too cute with a hint of her gooey chocolate s'more at the corner of her mouth. "Please don't let me keep you from getting up there on the dance floor." She nodded toward the cleared space with guests dancing, some as couples, others in friendship clusters. "Maybe you and Harper could take a spin."

Harper gagged, standing fast with her hand gripped on Maisey's pink paw-print leash. "I'll take Maisey for a walk and throw away the trash—staying in sight at all times, of course."

Swallowing a chuckle, he nodded and stacked their empty paper plates. "Sure, kiddo."

Zelda placed their plastic utensils in the disposable cups and set them on top of the plates. "Thank you. I'm sure Maisey will be glad to stretch her legs."

"Me, too," Harper said, balancing the trash, the leash looped around her hand.

He couldn't remember the last time she moved so quickly. Good to know she could still be motivated to do things. He watched his daughter meander over to the s'mores buffet and load up another for herself with one hand while keeping a secure hold of the leash on the other.

Turning back to Zelda, he resisted the urge to thumb away the chocolate. "How did it go today? Did Harper hold up her end of the workload?"

"She's got an incredible work ethic." Zelda swiped her mouth with a napkin. "Dog washing is tougher than it sounds, with all the lifting and keeping the dogs contained. She has a real gift with calming animals." Zelda cast a grin his way. "She must get that from you."

"We used to spend a lot of time together at the stables when she was little. I miss that." He paused, eyes catching on a young family with a toddler reaching up for her dad. Once, that would have been Harper. Now? Now his daughter ran away from him every chance she got. Nostalgia hit him, hard. "But I realize for whatever reason, she sees me as some kind of prison guard. At least with you, she can still have an outlet for her love of animals."

"You should have seen her bathing this skittish Dalmatian. She worked wonders soothing him. I found out afterward from the owner that the dog used to be a fire station mascot. The dog developed anxiety and got adopted by one of the firefighters."

Zelda adjusted her injured leg, bringing her almost imperceptibly closer. Unable to resist, he tracked the distance with interest.

"Now that sounds more like my girl who once bottle-fed a litter of kittens. Mowed lawns to raise money to help pay for vaccinations. Then made flyers and launched a campaign at school to get every one of them adopted." From behind them, he heard the unmistakable whisper of excited preteens debating with each other who could build the biggest s'mores.

"I love that story. We need more kids like that in the world." She pointed toward a cluster around a picnic table. "Look close and you'll see the Dalmatian asleep, all chilled out after his spa day—thanks to Harper."

In the shadows of the evening, he could make out a Dalmatian snoozing. Guests swirled around the dog, getting up to the dance floor in small groups. But the canine was completely unconcerned. He didn't even open his eyes. Pride welled inside Troy over his daughter's efforts. "I'd heard there was a first responders retreat coming in this week."

Zelda leaned back on her elbows, her chest straining against the soft cotton of her work T-shirt. "That's one of the things I love most about the Top Dog Dude Ranch, the way it's more than just a resort. Their focus on healing broken spirits shines through—and makes it a joy to get up for work in the morning."

He hoped some of that healing would rub off on his relationship with Harper. He couldn't deny that angle had offered all the more motivation to accept the summer job. A couple walked past the edge of their blanket, heads leaning toward each other as they made their way to the well-lit trail back to the cabins.

"Speaking of healing…" he said. "How's the search for relatives in the area going?"

"The initial names we looked into didn't net the hoped-for results, no relatives and no prospective donors," Zelda said, playing with the end of her braid. She rolled her dark locks between her fingertips, eyes going a bit distant as if lost in memory. "We've searched library records until we're cross-eyed. But there are some holes in the data because of a courthouse fire a couple of decades ago."

"That's right." Troy snapped his fingers. "I think I

heard someone mentioning it… Gil's dad maybe? The guy who makes the jewelry for the gift shop."

Zelda nodded. "He's a volunteer firefighter. I hear that citizens all up and down Main Street risked their lives hauling as much out as possible before the whole place went up in flames." She tipped her head to the side. "But then that's the spirit of the people here. Doing whatever's needed in a crisis. I'm hoping that same spirit will make a miracle for Lottie. Because nothing is more important right now."

He heard the caution—and the determination—in her voice, a tone he would do well to heed for himself. His focus needed to stay firmly on his daughter and building their future. "If you're okay here, I'll go pick up refills on our raspberry lemonade."

Letting the lively banjo strains wash over her, Zelda breathed in the crisp Moonlight Ridge air, hoping to dilute the distracting scent of Troy now that he'd wandered off to talk with his friends—after bringing her the promised lemonade refill. She had her life on track. She had no intention of rocking the boat.

Or should that phrase be more along the lines of not inviting ants to the picnic?

Regardless, the day had gone better than she'd expected with her injured ankle and her new helper. Even this outing with Troy had been easygoing—other than the occasional whiff of his spicy aftershave. The day felt mighty close to normal. Something she hadn't experienced in a very long time. There was something to the Top Dog healing and she wanted—needed—more of it, to be her strongest and best self to support her sister and niece. To be of assistance when for so long she'd felt helpless.

Her gaze gravitated to the group of children gathered under a sprawling tree, receiving last-minute notes and costume tweaks for their play. Under the glow of a string of lanterns, Lottie proudly sported a floral crown, so happy with her group of friends, children of the staff. The child's spirit was flourishing so much here, it was almost easy to forget how her body was failing her.

"Earth to Zelda," Isobel's voice cut through her musings as she lowered herself to sit beside her sibling. She waved her hand, her silver bangles clinking together. "How did the first day with Harper really go?"

Eyes flicking to where Harper now stood with Maisey beneath a big oak tree, Zelda considered the question. In the last rays of the sun slipping behind the mountains in the distance, Harper looked confident. Assured. Very much a young woman with a gift for animals she could hone into a career.

Zelda stirred her straw through her lemonade, dislodging the raspberries from under the crushed ice. "She's a hard worker. If she keeps up the pace, it would be worthwhile to keep her on even after my ankle heals."

Isobel raked a throw pillow into place behind her back, balancing her cup of lemonade. After adjusting her seat, her sister smoothed her black maxi dress. Beyond the confines of their blanket, a trio of kids raced back to their parents on a nearby quilt, s'more in hand.

"Keeping her around wouldn't have anything to do with spending more time with her dad?"

Neve arrived to sit on her other side, cradling a s'more on a napkin. Their professor sister always looked like she was about to drop into a class lecture—even at a casual barbecue dinner like tonight. Her hair was pulled back into a polished, slick high bun and two diamond studs mirrored stars in the low light of the bonfire. "Must be nice having your very own sexy-cowboy chauffer."

Around them, the crowd grew larger, louder as Raise the Woof played an old song everyone knew the words to. Laughter and singing echoed in the air.

Leaning back on her elbows, Zelda shot a side-eye at one sister, then the other. "I need to prerecord a disclaimer for you two that Troy and I are not a couple. We both have other goals for the summer, and then he's moving on."

Isobel fanned her face. "But all that chemistry."

Neve added, "And if he wasn't moving…"

Sighing, Zelda admitted, "There was a moment when we first met where the sparks were undeniable. But we talked about it. We agreed right after we first met that neither of us are in a good place for a relationship."

"I know, I know, but still…" Without looking at Zelda, Neve's stare cut straight through the crowd to where Troy stood by the drink refreshments.

One of the other cowboys had engaged him in conversation. Nothing escaped Neve's notice, part of her training as an academic, Zelda assumed. Though she'd been like that when they were kids, too—always noting patterns and tendencies, always categorizing.

Isobel said encouragingly, "Just keep an open mind."

"Even if I was in the market, my pride will not allow me to chase an off-limits guy." Zelda bumped her shoulder against Isobel's. "Just because you're all wrapped up in the warmth of new love doesn't mean it's out there for everyone."

Her sister had a rough go of it with her ex-husband, who'd used work as an excuse for bailing on co-parenting Lottie. Isobel had shouldered the weight of all those medical appointments and care by herself, while holding down a full-time career. If anyone deserved a happily-ever-after, Isobel did. And while Zelda knew there wasn't a limit on passing out happiness, she'd come to realize she needed to carve out that joy on her own first.

Rediscover herself. Because somehow, her identity had been swallowed up in the demands and selfishness of her partner until she hardly knew herself anymore.

Keeping track of his daughter was tougher than lassoing a calf in the ring. Out of breath, Troy refilled his raspberry lemonade for the third time before grabbing another napkin from the refreshments bar by the chuck wagon.

While Harper had stayed true to her promise to keep in sight with Maisey, she'd still pushed to the outer edges of the crowd, circling the whole perimeter. So much so that, at any moment, she could slip off into the forest if he looked away for even a moment.

A hand clapped him on the shoulder and he turned to find his boss.

Jacob nodded toward the stage. "Are you sticking around for the play?"

"Wouldn't miss it," Troy answered. "I've seen it every week since we arrived and somehow it never gets old."

Grinning, Jacob adjusted his Stetson. "We try to change up the presentation. The children's production is always a big hit, of course. The band is working on a musical version we're hoping to roll out later in the year."

From this distance, Troy could see Hollie plop a top hat onto their eldest son. The boy swiped the hat off, tossing it overhead and spinning around before catching it with his other hand. Such simple joy shone on Hollie and her son's face, even in the moments before a performance in front of strangers. Troy wished he could replicate that with his child.

His chest tightened. "I'm sure it will be top-notch."

Gil ducked into their conversation as he refilled his drink and snagged a cookie from the s'mores buffet. "My dad and I are helping out with painting new backdrops. Any chance you or your daughter has artistic talent?"

"Afraid not." He scanned the gathering, finally locating his daughter depositing Maisey back with Zelda.

Harper started to dart away again, but before she could make it a couple of feet, Hollie recruited her to help with the theater production. She linked arms with Harper, pointing to the small children lined up in a well-lit spot off the wooden dais. Hollie handed Harper puppy ears, a felt tail and some other props for the play.

Troy smiled, grateful for the unexpected help corralling his offspring. "Harper and I will have to drive over to see the new production."

Jacob swirled the ice of his drink before looking at Troy sidelong. Normally, his boss wore a smile the way that oak trees sported leaves. But now, hardened creases worked into his cheeks and furrowed his brow. "I heard the new intern is giving you some trouble?"

"He's a good worker," Troy answered evasively, more of that sympathy for the kid catching him unaware. Had Zelda's compassion for his daughter given him a wider lens where Wynn was concerned? Troy shuffled on his feet, kicking up some loose gravel as he straightened. "I'm just keeping a close eye on him when it comes to my daughter."

"Understood," Jacob said, nodding. "I have to confess I'm already sweating Ivy becoming a teen and she's got a few years left to go."

Gil tipped his elbow into Jacob's forearm. His gaze went to the stage. "Good thing she has all those older brothers to watch out for her."

Harper started to help put the costumes on the child actors, tying smocks around necks and adjusting flower-petal headbands. The kids still in their matching Top Dog Dude Ranch shirts began their storytelling transformation on a small stage in the middle of the ranch's town square.

Troy's throat moved in a slow swallow. "I just hope Zelda and her sisters can find a kidney donor for Lottie before she becomes a teenager—" Wincing, he paused. "I didn't mean to put a damper on things."

"Hey," Jacob said, "no apologies necessary. We're all here to help however we can."

Gil wiped the crumbs from his cookie on his jeans. "The summer festival event last month was a big help in growing the donor database for folks on the transplant list. I'm disappointed I wasn't a match."

Jacob pulled his Stetson from his head, placing it to his chest. "We're not stopping until we get the results Lottie needs. We're going to bring that Moonlight Ridge healing to that little girl one way or another."

The three men fell into silence while the band continued to play, the kind Troy recognized well as that guy-speak for the weight of emotions being too uncomfortable for words. Actions, tackling the problem was easier. But in this case, there was only so much they could do.

Raise the Woof had just finished a song when a high-pitched squeal from the stage microphone sent a hush through the crowd. As quick as the squawk of sound started, it settled and the folks around him took seats on benches, blankets and picnic tables, turning their attention from the live music to the upcoming production. Off to the left of the stage, the small children lined up. Hollie led the charge, but there was Harper, who knelt down next to the smallest child.

Man, he was thankful for the way the Top Dog folks were taking his daughter under their wing. Not just Zelda, but Hollie and Jacob, too.

The band roared with a drumroll. A wide spotlight cut through the dark, illuminating the stage.

Triplet boys holding tree branches ran onto the stage, then stood stock-still. Other children sat in a line in front of them, wearing flower masks.

Jacob and Hollie's oldest son, Freddy, wore a top hat and narrated, "Once upon a time, when my ancestors were settling into this area from Scotland and Ireland, they followed a doe to the cave opening. It wasn't just any old doe, though."

Hollie waved her hands, encouraging her young daughter to emerge on stage. With tentative steps, she made it to the center of the stage. A headband of white doe ears crowned the young girl's head.

Ivy adjusted her glasses as her brother continued, "The deer glowed like starlight. The Queen of the Forest."

As Ivy looked back off stage, he saw Harper give the young girl a thumbs-up. Ivy nodded and raised her chin high, seeming to calm down.

"My ancestors…" Freddy paused as one of his younger brothers walked in time with Harper.

They each grasped one of Lottie's wheelchair handles as they pushed her up a ramp. The light sound of wheels on wood reverberated as Freddy continued, his voice booming through the microphone system. Lottie's cherub face beamed as she joined the other children on stage. His daughter snuck back off stage, looping back around to where Hollie still stood watch over the children still yet to make their way into the spotlight.

Freddy waved his hands dramatically. "They knew the type of animal well. They used to roam Scotland and lead wayward souls to safe places and healing water."

Thumbing the brim of his top hat, Freddy continued, "They offered respite. A way to connect. You see, my ancestors were struggling to get settled into this region. Many challenges almost broke them. They wanted to give up on the land. On each other. But they followed the Queen of the Forest to the cave mouth."

Harper stepped into the full spotlight with a little boy wearing puppy ears balanced on her hip. He recognized the kid as the doctor's grandson. The boy's face was buried in Harper's side, suddenly shy. The crowd let out a collective coo, noting how sweet the scene was. Seeing his daughter so caring and responsible filled him with pride.

Freddy pulled a branch from his pocket, the sound of leaves whooshing through the air picked up by the microphone. Imitating a tree in a lively wind, Freddy pointed to another little boy with a branch. "There was a lost pup in the cave that needed attention. So, while they waited for a pot of coffee to brew over the fire, they cleaned up the young pup."

As he rustled the limb overhead, some of the leaves fell to the ground around him. "As they rinsed the puppy, their bond was renewed. Healed. They found a way to work with the land, with each other. Much like how our hot springs have healed and gathered people to this land for over a hundred years." Freddy took a deep breath before proclaiming, "We have a reputation for bringing people together because of it."

Harper bowed her head down to the little boy. Her lips moving in silence but he was able to read her lips: "It's your line, buddy."

The little fella's chest puffed with a deep inhale, puppy ears flopping as he popped up his head and shouted, "The end."

Troy whooped as the seated crowd rose to their feet. The gathered guests gave a standing ovation with whistles and claps echoing off the trees as the cast took a bow, Harper and Hollie, too. One of his daughter's rare smiles spread across her face as she balanced the "puppy" on her hip and held the hand of a little "sunflower."

Through the crowd, his gaze somehow found Zelda's where she'd gotten to her feet to balance on one crutch while she clapped. Was it his imagination, or did he feel a momentary tug of connection arc between them? He turned his attention back to the stage in a hurry.

This place was already working some of its legendary magic for his daughter, something he wouldn't take for granted. But he had to remember that his time here was short and Harper had already suffered enough loss. He needed to tread very warily in not letting her heart get broken.

And he shoved aside the niggling notion that he might also be protecting his own.

Chapter Seven

Zelda hadn't slept well. At all. Memories of the picnic evening with Troy kept her up all night, filled with nerves and confusion. She'd been isolated for so long, cut off from family and friends, she'd almost forgotten what the joy of a simple gathering could bring into her life. The sweetness of it all, the connection, made her hunger for more.

So why did it also leave her feeling anxious, like it couldn't possibly be real?

She knew she needed to dig deeper in her healing. To search inside for more answers about her last relationship so she didn't continue to make the same mistakes. But the toll of that personal accounting would take time and emotional resources that she didn't have while her focus needed to be on supporting her niece's search for a kidney donor. For now, she could only put one foot in front of the other—figuratively speaking, since she still had to work with her ankle propped.

"Thank you for your help with Maisey last night," Zelda said, working the furry knots out of Killian, a border collie who'd gone for an impromptu swim, followed by rolling in a pile of pine straw. Killian panted, her brown eyes patient as Zelda loosed one of the more twisted mats.

"Anytime," Harper responded, sweeping dog hair from the corner. She tightened her ponytail, sweat beading on her brow. Once on a task, Harper was dedicated. "She's a good girl. My mom's getting me a dog when she returns from Europe. She's visiting family, you know."

"What kind of dog are you getting?" And when was Troy's ex returning? The second unspoken question echoed in her mind, no matter how hard she tried to ignore it.

"Mom's bringing me a French bulldog—from France." Harper's chin tipped as she met Zelda's gaze defiantly, as if daring her to dispute it. After placing the broom back on the rack with a light *thunk*, Harper wiped her hands on her work apron.

Zelda hmm-ed in response, not sure what to say as getting a dog overseas sounded rather sus to her, but the girl was talking and Zelda didn't want to risk having the teen clam up. Something about her radiated an inner pain that called to the wounded core of Zelda.

Harper moved across the room, her sneakers squeaking as she passed Captain, the black male Great Dane drying. Captain chuffed at her as Harper gathered the two wet blue towels she'd used to wipe down the dog. "I asked for a girl puppy, but it's okay either way. As long as it's Parisian."

"Well, I've always wanted to go to France. Take a stroll down the Champs-Elysées while snacking on a fresh baguette, spend a whole week poring over every inch of the Louvre Museum. Watch the sunrise over the Seine." Zelda had almost forgotten that dream. But it was still buried deep inside her, a different vision for herself than the woman she had become in the previous year.

Harper smirked, tossing the towels into the paw-themed hamper. She scratched Captain's head. He leaned into her touch, giving her hand a lick. "Sounds like you need to start saving up your air miles."

Laughing, Zelda plucked a wad of fur from her brush before scooting her chair closer to Killian to get a better angle on his flank. "You have a good sense of humor."

Harper looked up fast, her eyes wide and her face... vulnerable. But she didn't speak.

The girl's surprise at the compliment tugged at Zelda's heart. "Did no one ever tell you that?"

Sniffing in pseudo dismissal, Harper grabbed a fresh pink towel and made her way back to Captain. Head downturned and shoulders slumping—a shadow of the confident young woman from moments before. "I'm not auditioning for a gig as a stand-up comedian."

Zelda looked away, carefully easing the border collie's front paw up for a nail trim, handling with care because holding too tight would just make Killian pull away. She suspected Harper was the same way. "What's your mom doing in France? Is it work related?"

"Family business," Harper said quickly and so convincingly that Zelda almost believed her. "She's visiting some cousin, a distant royal."

Royal? Surely there would have been some mention of that before now. It just sounded too farfetched—much like the French bulldog.

Zelda's worry ramped, but she kept her face open, using the breath work she'd relied on in the months after separating from her abusive ex to ground her now. Maybe it was nothing and Harper's story about her mom was true, but Zelda doubted it. Was the girl simply trying to get a reaction in some shock-jock fashion? Or was it a cry for help from a troubled teen?

Either way, it seemed like a red flag that should be shared with the person who knew her best. Zelda needed to have a more in-depth conversation with Troy about his daughter. The sooner the better.

Holding the door open to his pickup, Troy *had* to finish up this day. ASAP. No lingering for a picnic supper with the tempting Zelda. He needed to get his daughter home.

Harper piled in the back seat holding Maisey, while Zelda locked the grooming salon, maneuvering her crutches with ease now that she had more experience. Why couldn't he look away from her? She wasn't his usual type, but she was pretty in a way that said she didn't care what others thought. She dressed to please herself—today's work uniform accessorized with a neon pink head wrap and green rubber boots with a duck pattern.

Somehow that was far more attractive than any runway getup. He hadn't been able to get her out of his mind all afternoon. And that presented a problem.

Since she'd started working here a couple of months ago, he'd held firm to his plan of refraining from dating, not in the least tempted by any of the guests, even when some occasionally made their interest known.

Shaking free of the distraction, Troy adjusted the rearview mirror for a better view of his daughter. "How did it go today?"

"Fine," Harper said with a huff, folding her arms across her chest. The leather seat groaned as she slumped back.

He really needed to come up with some better questions to prompt her to talk, something that elicited more than a yes-or-no answer. Give him a horse, and he could understand every nuance of the communication. But person to person? More often than not, he struggled.

"How many dogs did you wash?" He flinched the instant the question came out of his mouth since that, too, would likely only elicit a one-word answer.

"Nine."

Maisey wagged her tail and licked Harper's face. His daughter looked down at the dog, a faint smile threatening the corners of her lips. Maisey circled on Harper's lap and then settled.

He scratched the back of his neck, searching for what to say next. Then he noticed Zelda making her way down the stone walkway and he welcomed the opportunity to abandon this going-nowhere conversation.

Jogging past the front bumper, Troy made it to the other side and waited, taking the moment to look at her without reservation. Zelda waved goodbye to a young couple with a border collie. They paused, the wife giving Zelda an appreciative hug as she pointed to her dog. Summer sunset illuminated the pink flush on Zelda's cheeks at what looked like was a heaping pile of compliments.

Beautiful.

The intensity of the thought rattled him. He knew better than to get invested in anyone right now, and yet something about Zelda kept pulling his thoughts to her. It wasn't like he didn't know how to deny himself a rogue physical attraction. But this was different. More.

He had never lived like a saint by any means. During his younger years on the rodeo circuit he'd deserved the bad rap he'd gained. Not so much anymore. He'd distanced himself from that time in his past.

Still, rumors took on a life of their own. Most of the time he didn't care. But once he'd gained full-time custody of his teenage daughter, he'd committed to making serious changes in his lifestyle. Buying a training camp would allow him to continue using the rodeo skills he loved, while spending less time on the road so he could be there for his kid. The plan had been solid.

Buying a facility required funding, however. And the interested financier needed to see he was worth the risk. So he found himself doing more and more to pull together the dream—sometimes at the expense of not seeing Harper as much.

Sure, he thrived on a challenge in the rodeo ring, but the stakes here were too high to live that lifestyle. His daughter was already acting out to the point of being picked up by the police for truancy last spring.

He would do whatever it took to give her the stability she deserved. So he would keep denying himself the draw of a certain charismatic dog groomer.

Tough as that challenge made every day lately.

Zelda cleared the end of the walkway and he reached for the door handle.

"Hey," Zelda said, her bright face a disconnect from the serious tone. She took a step back, half in the shadows of the sprawling pair of maple trees, bird feeders dangling made from upcycled tin dishes. "Could you wait a second? I have to ask you something. Privately."

He glanced over his shoulder at his daughter, finding her intent on texting with one hand and cradling Maisey with the other. He really should look into getting her a dog of her own. He'd never stayed in one place long enough to consider it before.

Returning his attention back to Zelda, he said, "Sure. What's on your mind?"

She dipped her head closer to his and whispered, her breath warmer than the summer breeze in the valley as it brushed against his cheek, "Could you take Harper home first so we can talk? I'm concerned about her. We can stay on your porch in case you're worried about her wandering off. I can get home on my own steam afterward." She adjusted her weight, the gravel shifting beneath her rain boots. "I promise."

He frowned, surprised. The gravity in her voice ramped up his own worries. Tucking his hand in his back jean pocket, he continued, "Sounds important. I hope she isn't giving you any trouble at the salon."

"No, no, of course not. Nothing like that. It may

not be important at all." She nibbled her bottom lip, eyes flitting to the family walking past them toward the main lodge.

A toddler babbled in the swaddle against his father's chest. Troy gave a slight nod and smile—the man and his wife had been on his family-friendly trail ride this morning. Zelda waved, too, a big smile crinkling her nose.

She turned back to him, the smile replaced with worry creases between her dark brows. "But just in case…"

"Better safe than sorry," he said, nodding at the concern swirling in her blue eyes. "Okay, no problem."

So much for keeping his distance. But Harper's well-being was top priority and he appreciated Zelda's extra care for his daughter.

After helping Zelda load into the front seat, he fired up the truck for their short—quiet—drive. The ride home checkered by the shade of tall trees, the radio humming with an old country tune. He glanced back in his rearview. Harper's delicate face awash with the blue glow of her screen. He turned the blinker on, pulling into the driveway of his cabin.

Harper straightened in the back seat, looking up with confusion as Troy parked the vehicle. "Aren't we taking Zelda home first?"

Zelda twisted to look over the back seat at her. "I decided I wanted the short walk outside with Maisey after being cooped up all day."

Harper eyed them suspiciously before shrugging and passing Maisey over to the front. "Sure. I guess I should look over the stuff for my SAT prep class tomorrow. So much for enjoying my day off."

The truck engine still rumbled, the air conditioner puffing on low since the summer altitude rarely grew too hot. Keeping the windows rolled up also offered more privacy, as he sat with Zelda's vanilla scent swirling through the truck cab. Each day, her scent, her very presence became ingrained deeper into his life.

He gripped the steering wheel to keep from reaching for her. Leather pressing into his palms and fingertips, he looked forward as Harper exited the truck. She disappeared into the cabin, door swinging behind her.

Only then did he turn toward Zelda. "What's on your mind?"

"Like I said," she said, chewing her bottom lip and toying with the end of her coffee-brown braid, "it may be nothing to worry about. But Zelda said something strange today. She mentioned that her mother is touring Europe and will be bringing her a French bulldog. I wouldn't have thought anything of it, except something about her demeanor had me questioning. Then she said her mother is over there visiting a cousin who is a distant royal… Is that true?"

Troy bit off a curse. "Not even remotely." He sighed. Hard. "Her mom is living in Arizona with her boyfriend."

"Oh no, Troy. I'm so sorry." She dropped her braid and clasped his hand.

Her touch soothed—and stirred all at once.

"She and I were over long ago. My heart is very much intact." Wary. But intact. "Although my anger runs high for my daughter, that she has to wake up every morning knowing that her mother abandoned her."

His thoughts spun as he tried to figure out his next steps with Harper. How did he even approach a conversation about this without appearing confrontational? Every day felt like he was in deeper over his head in this parenting gig.

"Harper's an incredible person," Zelda said with such intensity it warmed his heart. "You deserve to be proud of how you're guiding her through such a tough time."

He wasn't so sure about that part, but he didn't mind the encouragement after the rough go of it they'd had lately. "My summer job here was a godsend. I don't know how I would have managed if we'd been on the road. Everyone here has gone above and beyond to help make Harper feel welcome."

"But you miss the circuit."

Her words landed squarely, making him wonder how she'd gotten to know him so well. Not that there was any good to be found in lingering on that. He knew his way forward. "I'll miss it less once I have my training center open."

"I'll say it again, Troy." She squeezed his hand tighter, her forehead furrowed and earnest. "You're a good father. Involved. Loving. She's lucky to have you."

Her words reached to him and he met her gaze, holding. The air crackled between them with awareness, the blue of her eyes deepening, the rise and fall of her chest quickening as if in answer to the uptick in his heart rate. Memories of that single kiss between them last month filled him. Did that moment haunt her as well?

One hand still clasping hers, he reached with the other to brush back a stray lock of her hair, the silky texture gliding against his calloused fingertips. And against his better judgment, he wanted to kiss her again.

Ached to seal his mouth to hers, press her body against his. He angled forward, her breath hitching in the space between them before her mouth grazed his—

A noise from inside the cabin, the slamming of a door, broke the spell and he eased back with a ragged sigh. One she echoed.

He swept off his Stetson and thrust a hand through his hair, the delicate feel of her lips against his still burning like a brand. "Are you sure I can't drive you home?"

He cleared his throat to excise the deep rumble of longing that weighted the words.

"It's not that far to my place." She nodded toward her little cabin only a stone's throw away.

He dropped his Stetson back on his head and grasped the door handle. "Well, let me help you and Maisey out of the truck before I head inside to heat up leftovers for me and my trying daughter."

"I'm getting better with the crutches, but help with Maisey is still an offer I will gratefully accept."

He rounded the hood to her side of the pickup, using the time to draw in a couple of bracing breaths to slow his slugging heart. He opened her door and set the crutches against the quarter panel before reaching for Maisey, careful not to let his hand brush Zelda's soft chest.

Best not to even think about her chest.

He placed Maisey on the ground and secured the end of the leash to the gate before turning back to Zelda. As he extended his arms to her, she rested her hands on his shoulders. So naturally. Enticing. He lifted her, carefully, each inch closer rekindling the barely banked fire. She slid down the front of him, chest to chest until he eased her to the ground. She stood on one foot, the other crooked behind her as if they were in the middle of a kiss.

If they dared resume the kiss from a few moments prior. A risky proposition standing on his front lawn where Harper might see. She would have questions that he couldn't answer.

Clearing his throat, he stepped back and passed her the crutches. "I'll watch until you get home. Just to make sure you're safely inside."

"Thanks. Bye now," she said, her voice breathless, husky.

She looped Maisey's leash around her hand and started toward her cabin. His conscience pinched over not seeing her home, but true to her word, she was making easy progress along the path. Her braid swayed along her back, the late day sun casting dappled shadows over her.

Before he could second-guess himself, he jogged after her, drawing up alongside just as she reached her picket fence. He reached past her for the gate latch.

Her eyes widened in surprise. "Did I forget something?"

"Since Harper is going to her SAT prep class tomorrow and it's your day off, do you want to have lunch at the lodge?" The offer fell out of his mouth, barely planned, and yet, he held his breath waiting for her answer.

She shifted her weight onto one crutch, smiling apologetically. "I have plans."

Of course she did. He felt like a fool. A disappointed fool. "Sure, no worries—"

"But you're welcome to join me," she answered without hesitation.

"What kind of plans?"

"I'll let it be a surprise," she said with a playful glint in her eyes. "Unless you're afraid…"

He chuckled, never one to back down from a dare. Not that he needed much enticement to spend time with her. "Text me the time and I'll pick you up."

Harper's fingers flew across the keyboard of her cell to Wynn. Call me… I'm home… I miss you.

She waited. And waited. The screen stayed blank, not even the bubble of someone typing. Frustrated, she flung her phone onto the bed, where it bounced to rest beside a stuffed toy pony. Sighing, she stalked over to the window and flattened her palms to the panes, looking out over the front yard. Wishing she were anywhere but here, locked away from anything—anyone—fun.

The light still shone from the front porch. She could hear her father's voice and the low buzz of him talking to Zelda. Apparently her dad was the only one around here allowed to have friends. He'd driven away her mom somehow. Then he'd cut her off from Wynn, and now she wasn't even allowed to talk to Zelda without him checking up on her. Lying to people about her mom going to France felt a lot easier than telling anyone the truth about her messed-up life.

Her stomach swirling with frustration, Harper tugged the silky hair scrunchie from her ponytail and threw it to rest beside her cell. Her silent cell. She couldn't trust anyone.

The phone buzzed and she dived back across the room, landing on the bed on her belly. She grabbed the phone and rolled to her back. Not a message. A call. From Wynn. Her heart leaped.

She answered breathlessly. "Hey. Whatcha doing?"

Fingers yanking at the laces of her sneakers, she kicked off her shoes. They landed against the pine wood dresser, which had carvings of horses on the drawers. Her shoes rattled the photograph of her and her mom. It had been taken when she was six.

Before.

Back when things were good. Anger rumbled in her gut and tears threatened as the photograph frame plopped face down on the top of the dresser, wincing at the unmistakable sound of glass cracking. She left it there.

"Getting ready to eat supper." His voice sounded so familiar and yummy, like the best kind of song on her ears. "Uh, when are you and your father coming over?"

He wanted to see her? Her hopes took flight for a

fraction of a second before she recalled that a meal together wasn't a possibility tonight.

"Dad says we're eating leftovers at home." Ugh. She thought about the leftovers in the fridge. Barbecue, blue cheese coleslaw and corn fritters. Was it so wrong to want a trip to McDonald's and Starbucks with her friends?

"Oh, bummer."

He sounded so disappointed she wanted to race out to meet him. But her father had nailed her window closed and she couldn't escape out the front since he was busy flirting with Zelda.

She didn't even want to think about whom her mom might be with now. Hurt and betrayal rose in her throat, but she swallowed it down, focusing on the here and now instead of the raw emotions that threatened to swamp her if she dwelled on the fact that her mom had left.

Harper traced her fingers along the cool panes, looking out into the early night, more desperate than ever to see Wynn. "Are you at the dining hall?"

"Yeah, and they're having pizza and wings—" he paused for emphasis "—all you can eat."

Her mouth watered. It wasn't McDonald's, but... She sagged to sit on the end of her bed. She picked at the stitching on the green-and-white quilt. "I would sneak out and join you but my dad nailed my window closed."

"I'm not saying sneak over," he answered, explaining slowly. "I don't want your dad getting mad at me again. I don't think he'll give me a second chance. I was wondering if you *both* are coming to supper.

Your dad said if I saw you at the dining hall, I could eat with you guys."

"He did? Really?" She wasn't sure she believed that. It'd been a long time since he was her cool dad, the fun dad who'd brought her back the light blue Stetson from a rodeo championship. The bedazzled Stetson glinted on the hat rack across from her.

There'd been a time where her dad had been her hero, but she hadn't allowed herself to think about that for a long time, either. Things had changed. *He* had changed.

"I think he felt sorry for me," Wynn confided softly. "And for you."

Fat chance.

Padding across the rug, she flipped up the now-cracked picture of her mom and then removed her stackable silver rings. Tossing them into the Top Dog–themed horse show jewelry dish, she let out a sigh. "More like he figures he can keep his eye on us."

"Well, either way," Wynn brushed aside her skepticism, "do you think you can convince him you're dying to have pizza and wings?"

Looking around the room, which had mostly horse-themed decorations courtesy of the ranch, her eyes caught on the poster she'd hung of her favorite band next to her stand-up mirror. The poster of the girl group reminded her that there was a life outside this place.

She didn't even have to think twice about her answer to Wynn's invitation.

"I can sure try." And she wasn't giving up until her father agreed. Harper wanted to seize that opportunity—just like the poem she had read for class a few days ago had said to do. No one could say she wasn't learning with that kind of connection. "I'll text you when we're on our way."

After disconnecting the call, she grabbed her shoes and a fresh T-shirt, her favorite one she'd bought the last time her mom took her shopping. Right before she'd bailed for good.

Her mother had probably felt guilty for plotting a whole other life for herself behind their backs.

On second thought, Harper tossed aside the pity purchase and grabbed a simple leather shirt-vest instead. She climbed down the ladder from the loft, her conscience twinging over manipulating her father, but it was the only way she could see Wynn.

"Dad, do you want to go to supper together?"

Chapter Eight

Sitting by her cabin's dormant firepit, Zelda propped her foot on the cool stones while Maisey ambled around the fenced yard sniffing planters of petunias and gerbera daisies. She shouldn't be this excited about her plans with Troy tomorrow, but his "yes" had stirred a flurry of butterflies in her belly that rivaled the two taking flight from the potted plants. She smiled as her pup chased a monarch, entranced.

Adopting Maisey had been one of the best decisions Zelda ever made. The scruffy little one really did make for the best company. During Zelda's last dark months with her ex, the senior pup had helped Zelda keep her sanity, then gave her strength when she walked out and moved to Moonlight Ridge.

Tail held high, her dog trotted toward the peeling white-and-brown bark of the sycamore tree in her yard. Flopping down in the green grass brightened by last week's downpours, Maisey panted. She looked around, seeming to soak in the beauty of the dwindling sunlight. Zelda's heart squeezed as she noted the contentment in her dog's relaxed demeanor.

"Maisey, girl, do you miss your old life? The person

who loved you before?" It wasn't like Maisey knew her previous owners had abandoned her. Only that they'd left her life abruptly, leaving her at a shelter. But still...

"It's okay if you do. I understand how complicated love can be."

She didn't love her ex, but it had taken her a long time to detach her heart enough to see him realistically.

The rumbling of a truck firing to life carried on the wind. Squinting in the fading sunlight, she saw... Troy and Harper pulling away from their cabin, heading toward the lodge. Going to supper without her? He'd said they were going to eat leftovers.

Even as she told herself they just needed father-daughter time, she couldn't stop the sting at his misleading words that, now, left her feeling hurt. Rejected. He hadn't asked her to come along. It shouldn't matter, but somehow it did. She'd sensed a moment between them, or thought she had.

Apparently, she'd been wrong.

An old feeling of self-doubt stirred as she pressed her palms into the smooth gray stones beneath her. Was she really this bad at understanding intentions and interest?

Maisey trotted over and put her paws on the edge of the seat, her brown eyes wide and sympathetic. Zelda leaned forward to scratch her under the chin, then lifted her onto her lap.

"What do we care if he goes to supper without us?" Zelda smoothed a hand over Maisey's silky fur. Her pup leaned into the touch, arching her back. "It's not like I'm his responsibility. He brought me home. Duty done."

Face growing tight, she drew in shallow breaths as she watched the pickup fade from view down the road. Maisey yipped, drawing Zelda's attention back. A few head scratches elicited some gentle licks on her forearm.

Gathering her resolve and shoving the feeling of disappointment away, she looked back to the warm glow of her cabin. She set Maisey on the ground and shakily rose to her feet. Or rather, foot. Scooping the crutches propped up on the garden wall, she made a mental plan to salvage the evening.

"We'll just have us a nice girls' evening in together." Just like old times? She squelched the self-pitying thought as her hands wrapped around the light cushioning of the crutches. "We'll eat our favorite foods and I'll read a good book outside."

To be fair, Troy had been clear with her about his plans to stay single soon after she'd met him. Yes, he'd insisted his daughter was the reason. Now Zelda wondered if he still might have lingering feelings for his ex. Love and a broken heart could get all tangled up too easily.

All confusion aside, she knew one thing for sure. She would never be someone's consolation prize. She had her life and her confidence back. These days she lived to please herself and care for her family.

Wynn wondered if it would be too obvious to hang out in the lobby waiting for Harper. He didn't want to mess up the internship opportunity with her dad, but Troy had said eating together was okay.

Although Wynn's guilty conscience knew that invitation probably didn't include setting up a supper encounter.

Soft lights hummed in the peaks of the wooden ceiling. The sound of the lights mixed with the conversation of guests. Tapping his fingertips on the table, he inhaled the garlicky scents of pizza and buffalo wings as families came into the dining hall.

His stomach grumbled, but if he was already sitting, then he might miss his window to join Harper. He checked his phone for the third time—and to see if she'd texted. No message. And only fifteen minutes had passed since their conversation, but it felt longer. He shuffled from boot to boot, trying to decide what to do when a voice calling his name split through the fog.

Pivoting toward the dining hall, he scanned and found… The whitewater rafting instructor sitting with an old guy—in his fifties, maybe even sixties—at a table only a few feet away.

"Hey, Wynn," Gil called, motioning to an empty chair. "Come join me and my dad for supper."

After another glance at the front door—no Harper in sight—Wynn walked past a table full of maple cookies and Tennessee stack cakes before reaching Gil Hadley's table.

Sweeping off his Stetson, Wynn extended a hand in greeting. "Hello, sir." Then to Gil's father. "Good evening, Mr. Hadley."

The older man stood and shook his hand in a firm

grip. "Skip the Mr. Hadley stuff. Call me River Jack. Nice to meet you, Wynn. Please. Have a seat."

Might as well since it looked like Harper had stood him up. He put his hat on the table in front of the seat that would give him the best view of the entryway. "Thanks. I appreciate the invitation. I'll fill a plate and be right back."

Wynn made fast work of loading a dish, stacking three slices of different pizzas and adding a pile of wings before grabbing a bottle of Coke. Thank goodness the buffet allowed for unlimited trips.

Back at the table, he elbowed aside his hat and set down his food before claiming his seat.

Old Mr. Hadley—River Jack—chuckled, patting his stomach along the small paunch. "I sure miss the days when I could eat like that."

Gil chuckled, shifting the cup of sweet tea in his hand. "You should come join me on the water more often, Dad, and I'll help you work those calories off."

Wynn reached to the center of the table for the ranch dressing and a stack of napkins. "Mr. Gil, I didn't know your dad lived in the area."

River Jack swiped a wing through a blob of blue cheese. "I have my own place up the mountain, with a studio, but I'm having some work done." He leaned toward Wynn and whispered, "Problem with the plumbing."

Wynn leaned forward to hear the older man as the table full of children whooped with laughter. "What a lucky break that you can stay with your son."

He couldn't imagine wanting to hang out with his dad after leaving home for good.

Gil clapped his dad on the shoulder as chairs scraping against the floor echoed in the hall with a family reunion leaving the three tables behind them. "We're all each other has left."

River Jack swiped his napkin across his mouth, his eyes heavy. "My wife passed on a couple of years ago." With a shake of his head, he angled back. "Enough with that depressing talk. While I'm staying with my boy, I volunteered to lead a workshop in jewelry making. My way of giving back a bit to the ranch and their good work."

Wynn looked up from his food, realizing... River Jack. Gems by River Jack. "Um, I've seen some of your pieces in the shop. They're really pretty."

He'd wanted to get something for Harper, a pair of pink crystal earrings, but he didn't have the money.

"Thanks," River Jack said. "Are you enjoying your internship here? Made any friends?"

Wynn couldn't stop himself from checking the entryway and buffet line for probably the millionth time, except this time was the winner. Harper loaded her plate, a step ahead of her dad. When had she arrived and how had he missed her?

He'd forgotten to check his texts since he'd been trying to devote his attention to the conversation at the tables. He liked to think his manners were passable even though he struggled at school.

But now, Harper was here.

Embodying his every dream, she looked hot in a

simple leather vest and jeans. He couldn't take his eyes off of her now.

Wynn hauled his gaze away back to the conversation. "Mr. Shaw is a good boss. And his daughter's nice."

Gil nodded toward the pizza warmer. "And there they are. Do you mind if we invite them to join us?"

"Not at all," Wynn said. In fact, he couldn't have planned it better if he'd tried. Troy couldn't possibly suspect him or Harper now.

Gil stood, waving. "Shaw? Come join us." He dragged a chair over to add to the other empty one at the table. "We have room."

Harper walked in front of her dad, balancing the plate, her smile wide and just for him. Thankfully her dad was behind her and couldn't see, although that kept Wynn from being able to smile back with a wink. He hoped she saw the happiness in his eyes as he leaped to his feet and held out her chair for her.

Her dark blond hair brushed the back of his hand as she sat, so silky he could still feel it even after he returned to his seat. Then Gil, his dad and Troy talked and Wynn was happy to let them, enjoying just getting to be with Harper, to look at her and not worry about being found out. Her knee brushed his under the table and he almost choked on his pepperoni pizza. He dropped the piece on his plate and grabbed his soda for a big, draining gulp.

"Um," he said, coughing again. "I'm going to get another Coke."

Harper scraped back her chair. "Hold on. I'll come with you and check out the desserts."

Without waiting for her dad to argue, Wynn turned on his bootheel and made his way to the soda table and sundae-making station with Harper keeping up with him step for step. They waited in line behind two tweens chatting about getting their braces off soon. Almost on instinct, Wynn stopped smiling, suddenly conscious of his slightly crooked bottom teeth. His dad said they couldn't afford braces.

Harper picked up a sundae mug and handed it to him. As he took the crystal bowl, his own insecurities melted away when Harper's wide smile made her eyes so bright.

Angling closer to him, Harper whispered, "I should have known they would have barbecue pizza, too."

"It wasn't bad, really," he said. "Although I liked the pepperoni best."

She grinned, adding a scoop of vanilla bean ice cream into the base of her sundae bowl. And then plopped another scoop into his before moving toward the sprinkles. "I'll pass on that one. Give me good old cheese pizza any day of the week."

Wynn glanced back over his shoulder, relieved to find Troy deep in conversation with the two guys at the table. "Was it tough to convince your dad to come?"

"Not at all," she said, her voice surprised. Absently, she added a heaping pile of rainbow sprinkles to her bowl. Wynn waved his hand as she pointed to the bowl of berries. "He seemed glad—surprised—that I suggested it. I feel a little guilty."

He winced, filling a soda glass and trying to figure out what the crinkle between her brow was about. He was so used to disappointing people. "Are you mad at me for asking?"

"You know better than that." Harper smiled, brushing her shoulder against him. "He looked really happy over supper. Maybe it wouldn't be so bad if I ask him to bring me to dinner again tomorrow."

A jolt of victory kicked through him, like maybe things were finally going his way. Balancing his soda in one hand and his Harper-made sundae in the other, he walked taller back to their table.

As he took his seat, Hollie O'Brien spoke into a microphone, calling out to the diners, "Please continue to eat as long as you like. Meanwhile, welcome to one of our simple—my favorite—pack-tivities. Game night! There's no requirement to stay with your own party. If you're flying solo this evening, find an empty chair and join others. Rodeo-opoly, our own version of Clue, Western style, and, of course, cards."

Hollie took her place behind the table lined with games, helping the fast-forming line of people each find the perfect fit.

River Jack leaned back in his chair, tossing his napkin on the table. "Are you staying for game night?"

Troy scratched the back of his neck. "I'm not sure that's quite my daughter's speed—"

Harper grabbed her father's elbow. "I'd love to, Dad. Pictionary is my favorite."

Pictionary?

The choice landed in Wynn's gut with a thud. He'd

been hoping for something like Yahtzee or cards. Anything with numbers, rather than words he may not understand.

With a creeping dread, Wynn pushed aside his uneaten ice cream. "Actually, I should call it a night. I had a long day and work starts early. Don't want to disappoint my boss."

Disappointment flooded Harper's face and he hated that he'd let her down. He hated even more that he couldn't manage a simple kids' game with the girl he wanted to impress.

Feeling lower than low, he grabbed his soda and made fast tracks out of the dining hall and back to the bunkhouse.

Just when he thought he had his sea legs under him, Troy felt the world shift. One look at Zelda when he picked her up for their outing just about knocked him flat.

Settled behind the wheel with Zelda beside him, he cranked the engine and tried to keep his eyes off the sight of her. But the image of her remained burned into his brain.

Sun washed over her. She looked far too enticing in the long golden skirt that flowed down to her ankles. The tight faded blue tank fit her curves. His breath caught in his chest, his heart hammering.

He scrubbed a hand over his face. At least with Harper at her SAT prep class, he could rest easy and enjoy a morning with Zelda. Although the plans still stayed a mystery. "So where are we headed for this mystery outing?"

"To the greenhouse." She smoothed her hands along her gold flowy skirt.

Was it his imagination, or did she seem a bit cooler than usual? Those heated moments in his truck from the night before had wreaked havoc on his brain all night long. Yet Harper's demeanor today seemed a little off.

Maybe she'd been second-guessing that time.

"For lunch?" He steered the truck onto the narrow road leading from the cabins toward the main lodge.

She finally grinned, crinkling her nose, blue eyes as bright as the mountain sky. "For craft day. With food served too."

He schooled his features to stay neutral. "Crafts? Like, uh, woodworking? Carving?"

She tipped her chin. "It's a surprise. Unless you're afraid…"

There was a fire in her today. There'd always been a spark between them, but rather than drawing them closer now, she seemed to be holding him at arm's length. He wasn't sure why. And he definitely wasn't sure why it bothered him when he needed to keep things…platonic.

At least his dinner last night with his daughter had been a success. Wynn hadn't even stuck around pushing the time together to the limit. Maybe the old adage about parental approval being the kiss of death for a teenage relationship was true. At least one mystery would be solved soon with the specifics of this craft outing.

Even driving slowly along the narrow ranch road, they arrived outside the massive greenhouse in short order. The dirt parking lot outside was full with other attendees walking over from their cabins. Apparently, this was a popular pack-tivity.

Once he'd parked his truck between two pines, he grasped Zelda's elbow to help her out, walking alongside her past flats of flowers, a gurgling fountain and stacks of mulch. Small concrete statues were tucked along the way, small dogs and fairies. Over the door, a sign proclaimed Grow Where You Are Planted.

Words to live by.

Inside, the scent of earth and plant life filled the air. Grow lights hummed overhead, casting a warm glow over rows of flowers and greenery, from lilacs to ferns. Potted plants flourished in stands. Bundles of drying herbs and blooms hung upside down from hooks.

He strode past a gurgling fountain made of a rustic pump flowing into an overlarge bucket toward two lengthy tables set up in back, already surrounded by guests. But he also saw staff, like the ranch owner Hollie and the stable manager, Eliza.

He recognized another face as well—none other than River Jack. "Welcome, Troy. Glad to see you here, although I didn't expect to find you at a workshop to make jewelry and dream catchers."

Troy took in the supplies on the tables with a new perspective. Wooden circles, pre-strung with twine, ready to decorate. Bins of supplies lined the table—

feathers, ribbons, leather cords, dried flowers and greenery. And in the center, a large bowl of crystals and beads.

He scanned over the corner table with sandwiches, chips, cookies, and bottled drinks before taking in the rest of crowd. The room was full of mostly female participants, other than River Jack and an older gentleman wearing a British flag shirt, sitting beside someone who appeared to be his wife.

Troy rubbed his palms together. "Well, time to channel my creativity and make what will probably be the world's ugliest dream catcher."

Laughter rippled through the group as they took their seats. He didn't much like the way the guest in the flag shirt was eying Zelda. Troy stepped between them to hold out her chair for her. She smiled her thanks over her shoulder.

Her blue eyes caught and held his, making his head swim as he took his seat beside her. The brush of her skirt against his leg scrambled his brain until he barely registered the instructions.

Troy shifted his focus to River Jack as he raised a sun-weathered hand in a grand gesture.

"Jewelry is about more than just decoration. Each piece carries emotions and, yes, even dreams. My wife and I were high school friends then sweethearts. I went from making her jewelry out of flowers to mining my own crystals."

Hollie adjusted her dark ponytail. She picked up several wooden craft bins and began distributing them to the group. "Friends to lovers," she said with a fond smile. "That reminds me of a couple who came for Christmas. His fiancée ditched him right before the trip, so he invited his best friend and her toddler to come with them."

The wistful look on the faces of at least half the room gave him only a moment's warning that the floodgates of romantic memories were about to be opened.

Susanna, the school librarian, was the next to pipe up. She wound sky blue suede around the small metal hoop as she shared with the British couple across the table. "My husband, Micah, and I connected at the back-to-school night for his nephew. Benji was struggling with his reading. I ended up tutoring him for the summer to earn extra money for my school loans. And the rest is history."

The stable manager—Eliza—arranged crystal beads into a pattern on the table in front of her, helping the harried mom beside her who was juggling projects for two young daughters. "Nolan and I met when his granddaughter needed goat's milk. It's funny how such a simple moment can be so life-changing."

A dreamy sigh drew all eyes to the ranch's head landscaper, Charlotte, lounging in the doorway leading to her office. Behind her, the space held a cluttered desk. The wall was full of sketches and plans for future landscape designs at the ranch.

Charlotte shrugged, flipping her long blond hair over her shoulder as she smiled at a cluster of mothers and adult daughters from a family reunion. "What can I say? One look at Declan in that cop's uniform and I was toast."

She fanned her face with a gloved hand, a faint blush painting her pale cheeks.

On and on it went between crafting and eating, with guests sharing—a college proposal, a chance meeting on an airplane, matchmaking children—until he couldn't help but notice Zelda drawing inward, focusing more and more intently on threading beads into a delicate bracelet with each lovey-dovey revelation.

She didn't look up from her work, her expression closed. So he focused on the dream catcher he'd started and let the minutes tick by. Stringing the dark brown embroidery floss around the hoop in a passable pattern, he shifted in his seat, searching for something to deflect the tension that seemed to pull between them today.

But at the same moment an older woman with a necklace full of grandchildren charms leaned toward them and interrupted to ask Troy, "How did you meet your daughter's mom?"

Troy winced.

Susanna gasped and elbowed her gently. "Ma'am, they're divorced."

The grandmother clutched her clinking necklace. She looked down, shifting stray beads in front of her. "Oh, I thought she died."

Like that made her question any better? But at least it shut down the talk of cupid's arrows.

He grabbed a handful of dark black obsidian stones and set to work on decorating his dream catcher all the faster as—thankfully—the other workshop attendees settled back into fine-tuning their own creations.

Zelda angled toward him, her shoulder brushing his as she whispered, "I'm sorry about that. Some people are just clueless."

Her breath was warm and soft against his ear. No matter what tension he'd felt between them earlier, he appreciated that she remained as kindhearted as always. Because beneath the attraction he felt toward her was the ever-present knowledge that she was a good person.

"You have nothing to apologize for." Troy thumbed the yellow-and-brown feather in his hand before attaching it to the embroidery floss. The project was coming together better than he'd expected, even if he was finishing up a bit slower than others.

The room grew quieter as some of the attendees gathered their projects to leave, oohing and aahing on their way out. The swishing of the door let in gusts of fresh air, stirring hints of glitter on the table.

"Well, I'm sorry to have dragged you along." Her face softened, fingers working nimbly as she tied off the thin string of the glittering bracelet. "If I'd have realized they would all be playing matchmaker, I would have come up with a different plan."

"They mean well. And I had the chance to make this."

He lifted his dream catcher off the table and let it catch in the soft light of the workspace. Dark leather wound around the hoop and the obsidian stones he selected formed the innermost circle. Dark feathers cascaded from strings at the bottom.

All those years of braiding horsetails and manes for shows had paid off on this craft in an unexpected way. "It didn't turn out too bad, if I do say so myself."

Her smile lit her eyes, glinting like the dangling crystals. "Harper will love it."

"Actually, I made it for you," he said impulsively, nudging it along the table toward her. "As a thanks for all you've done for my girl. Although it's not much to look at."

"It's adorable." She pressed her hands to the dream catcher with reverence. "You've thanked me plenty."

He searched for the words to express how much it meant to him that Zelda had reached out to his child during such a vulnerable time. While no one could replace Harper's mom, or fill that void, having the attention and affirmation of an adult female had already softened the edges of his daughter's anger.

Leaning closer, he found himself whispering, "About the kiss…"

"Which one?" she asked with a soft laugh.

He grinned. "The most recent."

Just that fast the air between them shifted from lighthearted to electric, sparking with memories of both times, along with a yearning for a repeat. No question his need was echoed in her eyes.

Her fingers closed around the dream catcher. "Are you trying to change the rules we set in place? Because I thought we both agreed this was a bad time for a relationship."

She spoke the truth. He recognized it even as something within him fought against the practical boundaries he'd carefully installed around himself.

"I guess a quiet affair is out of the question," he said dryly without thinking.

Her eyebrows shot upward in surprise, but she stayed silent for a beat, the idea taking shape and form between them. And in that silence, he wondered if there was some possible way to make that simple, reckless utterance a reality that wouldn't blow up their lives.

Chapter Nine

Her head spinning, Zelda couldn't even come up with a reply to Troy's outlandish statement. Surely he was joking about having an affair. Not that she could even question him here with the scattering of lingering attendees finishing their crafts and sandwiches while River Jack packed away his gems.

But make no mistake, she needed to set the record straight.

A low rumble of thunder rolled in the distance as she turned her attention to her workstation, putting feathers, blue crystals and leftover suede leather strands into the clearly labeled wooden bins. Zelda hitched her backpack in place and tucked her crutches under her arms, feeling rattled. So scattered she almost forgot her dream catcher, then couldn't figure out how to carry it. Thankfully, Troy picked it up, ever thoughtful.

She swallowed down a lump in her throat, hoping to settle her jangled nerves. "Goodbye, everyone. It's been fun but I need to check on Maisey, and Troy has to pick up his daughter."

With each awkward amble across the greenhouse and through the door, she cursed the crutches that limited her freedom. Hopefully, not for much longer. Her ankle hurt, but it was feeling better. She'd wrapped it tightly this morning. She was even managing to get around the cabin on her own. Although moving this quickly? She felt a twinge with each step.

She focused forward, eyes locked on Troy's truck parked in the dirt lot, just past flats of mountain laurels and purple passionflowers. While the sun valiantly fought to peek through the gathering storm, puddles still began to form with the light drizzle, creating a mini obstacle course, which she diligently moved through carefully. Troy's steps echoed behind her, his shadow stretching over and past her until he pulled up alongside her at the pickup.

He held up his dream catcher and her beaded bracelet. "You still haven't answered my question."

She pitched her crutches into the truck bed and pivoted to face him. Rain droplets rolled down her cheeks. "You are out of your mind."

A dimple creased his cheek, crinkles fanning from his brown eyes. "Not too worried about my ego, are you?"

"Not in the least." She braced a hand on the quarter panel, lifting up her injured ankle. "And it's not as if you're serious. If I recall, you're looking for a reputation makeover rather than a buckle bunny hookup."

She bit her lip at the last words, regretting her outburst as they drew the gaze of passersby.

"Zelda, honey," he said, his face flooding with remorse. "I'm sorry. I shouldn't have joked about something like that."

Setting their crafts on the back seat, then stepping closer, he stroked her dampening hair, and heaven help her, she swayed toward him, wondering for a moment if she dared steal one covert encounter for herself. But as quickly as the thought—the desire—flickered through her, she remembered her vow to guard her heart, because something about this man tempted her far too much.

She pressed a palm to his chest, her fingertips absorbing the warmth of cotton and the steel of muscles. "Troy, I apologize if I hurt your feelings or wounded your ego, but we both know this can't lead anywhere—"

A shout from across the parking lot cut her short. Waving, a man called out for Troy. She pivoted fast, stumbling for balance and slamming against Troy's chest. His arms wrapped around her, steadying. Although his jaw clenched and a low curse slipped from his mouth.

What was wrong? Had she stepped on his foot? Or accidentally elbowed him?

The man strode closer, wearing pristine boots, a crisp Stetson and a mustache that sported a speckling of gray. "Well, hello there, Shaw. I've been looking all over this fancy spread for you. I decided to pop in and take a look-see at your junior rodeo practice this afternoon." He paused, sweeping his Stetson from his head. "And who is this pretty little lady with you?"

Troy's shoulders braced, his face tense with a forced smile. "Zelda, this is Levi Bowen, the primary investor

in my training center. Levi, this is Zelda Dalton. She's
a talented dog groomer here at the ranch."

The introduction proved as chilling as a bucket of
ice water. Keeping their distance was about more than
just protecting Harper's feelings. Troy's very liveli-
hood was in the balance. She recalled all too well the
importance of Levi Bowen to Troy's future.

Clearing her throat, she thrust out her hand. "Nice
to meet you. Troy's being a good neighbor and giving
me a ride home since I injured my ankle." She opened
the truck door. "I'll wait in the pickup while the two
of you talk shop."

Troy wished he'd received advance warning of Levi
Bowen's visit, but at least his financier had made the
trip to the Top Dog Dude Ranch. He was showing an
interest. And heaven knew, this afternoon's schedule
was packed, due to taking a half day off for crafting.

Still, Troy was thankful to have time to connect with
his potential investor, to explain where the Top Dog
facilities were located, and hopefully set up a phone
call for later in the week.

He'd taken Zelda home in one of the most silent
and awkward rides of his life. She'd bolted out of his
pickup, barely using the crutches as she fast-tracked
into her cabin. He would need to speak with her later.

The delay was a good thing, though, as it would
give him time to get his head and thoughts together.
For a reason he couldn't define, he hung the dream
catcher on a picket of her fence before climbing back
into his truck to gather his daughter from SAT prep

at the ranch's little library annex, ever aware of Levi following in his own vehicle.

Now, Harper darted past him into the indoor arena as he ushered Levi inside. He wondered if she understood how important this moment was for him. For them both. For their future. But she looked happy, so the last thing he wanted was to upset that applecart. Especially in front of Levi.

Troy tucked his hands in his back pockets. "This is where we'll hold the junior rodeo. You'll see some of our young stars practicing today, but you'll also get a bird's-eye view of the ranch's kids' camp that I've been leading over the summer."

The indoor arena was attached to the main stable, a perfect space for a small rodeo. He'd heard the structure had also been used for harvest festivals and Christmas pageants. The ranch staged large wedding receptions in the place.

Overhead lights showcased the young competitors off to his left. About five tweens practiced their roping skills on model cows. He noted the way Wynn gave Harper a leg up onto one of the Top Dog mares before mounting his own horse. He hadn't seen Harper ride in a long time. But there she was, lined up behind Rory, the landscaper's teenaged brother, waiting to take a turn at barrels.

Troy gave Levi a moment to soak it all in. Actions often spoke louder than words. Eliza, the stable manager, knew how to command space and coax even the youngest and most inexperienced kid campers interested in horses. A wide smile spreading across her face, she was teaching them a song about horse care. At the center of the circle of children, her call-and-response song ended in a swell of cheers. Lottie's bell-like laughter echoed the loudest and he couldn't help his thoughts from wandering to Zelda.

Levi stroked his mustache, surveying the airy space. He paused as he watched one of the older teens tighten a girth on a black-and-white paint horse. "Nice, nice, and quite a significant addition for a family-run business."

"I've appreciated the front-row seat to see how they develop their business. The O'Briens have even expanded to a second location over on the other side of the state—at an old dairy farm. I plan to check that out soon myself to see if there are any new ideas I can implement at my own facility."

"Creative use of property." Levi adjusted his Stetson as they stopped in front of where the track for pole bending was being set up by the ranch hands. Each pole needed to be set up twenty-one feet apart. Horse and rider had to weave through the course in the least amount of time. He nodded his approval as the ranch hands carefully aligned the course. "How much longer until you sign the contract on the property you're planning to lease?"

"September." He hoped. Provided the money came through. He didn't want to subject Harper to a move mid-school year, especially after so much upheaval.

"It's a shame the training facility can't be closer to this place. I wouldn't mind booking a cabin when I come to visit." An eight-year-old boy with close-cropped hair walked by them, dropping his small lasso. Levi crouched down to pick up the rope and hand it back to the kid, earning a high five of thanks. "How's your daughter going to take moving again?"

Troy's gaze shot to Harper, whose form was nearly perfect as she galloped back to where Wynn let out a whoop of approval. "I'm homeschooling her until we get settled so there's less change."

"Wow." Levi's eyes went wide. "You really are committed to leaving your old rambling ways behind."

He ignored the stir of defensiveness since his commitment to Harper had never been in question for an instant.

"I'm dedicated to doing whatever it takes to help my daughter." Even giving up his life's dream. Even sucking up to a rich financier who inherited his fortune. As quickly as the thought slipped into his mind, he shoved it aside. Levi didn't deserve his resentment.

Levi clapped him on the shoulder. "So, what's the deal with the lady you were with earlier?"

Troy wished he knew. They'd been interrupted in the middle of the one of the most compelling conversations of his life. But he settled for a simpler reply.

"My daughter works for her at the dog grooming salon, so we cross paths a good bit." The words sounded like a weak excuse even to his own ears, even knowing they were true—just not the whole story. His skin burned, not from embarrassment but rather the impending sense of doom, that his plans might be about to go up in smoke.

Levi nodded, stroking his mustache thoughtfully.

"Well, I'm pleased to see you're settling down with a nice young lady. You make a nice couple."

Troy's head whipped around as surprise rocked through him. He couldn't have heard what he just thought. Levi had misunderstood the relationship with Zelda in a way that wasn't fair to her in the least. All joking aside about a no-strings affair, Troy respected her too much to use her for his own gain.

Opening his mouth to correct Levi's misunderstanding, Troy was stopped short by a tween girl with a blond ponytail and black helmet tacking up a palomino. Two kids—maybe five and seven—were playing some sort of game where they were zipping around behind her horse and shrieking. A recipe for a spooked mount and broken bones if he ever saw one. Waving to Levi with a promise to be right back, Troy jogged over to stop the boys from getting seriously hurt.

But without question, he would be setting the record straight with Levi—and with Zelda.

Zelda welcomed the distraction of stuffing information packets with her sisters for Lottie's next donor drive, scheduled for the junior rodeo in two weeks. She tried—and mostly failed—to keep her mind off remembering the shock on Troy's face when he'd seen his potential financier walking toward them.

On the stocky oak dining table turned command center, they organized piles of flyers, contact forms and little key chains with the website for the national donor registry. She trifolded the brochures, one after the other, taking comfort in the routine, like using a fidget spinner to calm nerves.

Isobel's cabin, more spacious than Zelda's and Neve's, sported the rustic beauty of a stone fireplace, stretching to the high ceiling, an antler chandelier sprawling over the mantel. Log walls and pine and leather furniture rounded out the decor. But more than just larger, the space sported accommodations for Lottie's wheelchair.

The doors were wider for a wheelchair to navigate, and the kitchen counter was lower in places where Lottie could roll right up without having to reach awkwardly. The bathrooms sported rails and an accessible shower. And the list went on and on. Such simple— and crucial—additions that could make or break a trip for Lottie.

Zelda's fist clenched around a box of key chains. A twinge of guilt shot through her over not having been more of a help to her sister over the years, even though she had tried since arriving here, especially early on like with taking Lottie to her equine therapy classes led by Troy.

Zelda stifled a groan of frustration as once again, her thoughts had spiraled back to Troy, an increasingly common occurrence...

When Zelda had volunteered to take Lottie on an outing, she definitely hadn't counted on her niece choosing equine therapy with rodeo hotshot Troy Shaw.

At least, so far, he was nowhere in sight in the stable yard. A split rail fence sectioned off a corral for the young riders. Top Dog staff guided the children on ponies and small horses in a circle, one person with each rider. Even her understandably protective sister would approve.

Zelda snapped a photo of Lottie on a Shetland pony with flowers woven into the mane. The adaptive saddle steadied her on either side, her pink cowgirl hat perched on her head with pride.

Tucking her cell into her back pocket, Zelda reclaimed her Yeti full of dark roast from the ground by her feet. Her new cowgirl boots were pinching her toes, but she intended to get use out of the overpriced purchase she really couldn't afford, especially since she spent most of the day in rubber boots washing dogs.

Neve had wandered off to check out the petting zoo, under the auspices of finding the gentlest creatures to meet Lottie. Zelda knew Neve really just wanted an excuse to hang out with the animals. Growing up, she would wander in the woods for hours, often returning with a wounded creature.

"Hey, beautiful," a deep voice rumbled from behind her, an instant before Troy pulled up beside her to lean a lazy hip against the fence post. "How was your day washing pooches?"

Her shoulders tensed and she cut a sideways glance at him, trying not to notice his long legs in crisp denim. "I think you're paying me a compliment, but saying something nice about a person's looks isn't really saying much of substance. Appearance is beyond our control."

She was quite proud of her speech, given her tongue

*threatened to stick to the roof of her mouth like she'd
eaten peanut butter with nothing to drink. She hated,
hated, hated that her ex had left her with these insecurities around men.*

*"Fair enough." He knuckled his Stetson up, reveal-
ing a hint of dark hair. "So is your sister some kind
of Dr. Dolittle?"*

Zelda startled. "What do you mean?"

*"Your sister, over there." He gestured toward the
pigpen, where Neve crouched talking between the
slats. "She's been chattering away to all the animals
in the barn this morning."*

*Was he interested in her sister? Well, Neve was wel-
come to him. "Oh, yes, she's a wildlife biologist. She's
always preferred critters to people."*

*A half smile kicked a dimple into one tanned cheek.
"I can't say that I blame her."*

*She pivoted to face him full-on. "Do I take that
to mean you're interested? Because if you're looking for me to supply the inside track on my own flesh
and blood for some rodeo stud, then you're sadly mistaken."*

*He turned up the grin to full wattage. "You think
I'm a stud?"*

*Oh heavens. She rolled her eyes. "I think you're
insufferable."*

Neve would shut him down in three seconds flat.

"But you're not walking away."

*"Oh, I can rectify that." She hugged her Yeti to her
chest and started walking. She didn't know where she*

was going since she'd promised to keep Lottie within
eyesight. But her sore, booted feet were moving.

"Hey," Troy called out, "hold up." He jogged across
the arena, catching up in a half-dozen long strides.

Stopping in her tracks, she hitched her hands on
her hips. "Clearly I did not deflate your overblown
ego enough if you're back for more."

"I apologize." He swept off his Stetson, smacking it
against the side of his leg. "I thought we were...uh...
bantering?"

He wasn't wrong. And from the looks of things, he
wasn't interested in Neve after all.

Zelda sighed. "I'm not a buckle bunny looking for
a hookup."

"I don't recall asking you," he said with a quirked
eyebrow.

"Oh." She wasn't speechless often. She didn't like
what that said about his appeal.

"Right. We're both new here at the ranch." He
searched the sky as if looking for the right words before he swiped an arm across his forehead and plunked
his hat in place again. "I was making conversation,
and yes, I fell into old habits. I apologize for stepping
out of line. I'll try to do better going forward."

Was he genuine? Or a player? She didn't know and
it honestly didn't matter. Because even if her boots
weren't made for walking, the last thing she needed
was even a hint of a romantic entanglement. "Apology accepted. Now don't let me keep you from work."

She turned her attention back to Lottie and made a
beeline in her niece's direction. And with every pain-

ful step, she reminded herself that blisters on her heels weren't nearly as painful as the ones on her heart...

Zelda pushed aside thoughts from her early days at the ranch and focused on stuffing information folders. At least she'd found time to research a few more potential leads to finding Gran's son while she was at her computer the night before. The leads had been dead ends, but the more avenues they eliminated, the closer they came to uncovering the identity of that much-needed donor possibility for Lottie.

Isobel walked over from the kitchen, holding a tray with their lunch—fried catfish sandwiches, hushpuppies and moonshine cookies.

Neve pointed to the dream catcher Zelda had plucked from her picket fence on her way over. "Did you make that?"

Zelda shook her head. "I made a friendship bracelet."

"Oh." Isobel sighed in relief, as she set the tray down on the only spare bit of wood on the tabletop. "One of the kids gave the dreamcatcher to you. That's sweet."

"Um, actually," Zelda said, tracing the obsidian rocks on the design, remembering the way the cowboy carefully wove the strands together, "Troy made it. I'll be sure to let him know your 'verdict' on his crafting skills."

Her two sisters exchanged knowing looks before returning to their tasks in between bites of their catfish sandwiches.

Neve secured pens to five clipboards, her dark hair

sliding forward as she leaned to reach into the box under the table. "Well, regardless, I'm disappointed I missed out on the dream catcher workshop. It's always a winner."

Isobel grabbed a cookie from the small pile. After taking a nibble, she gestured toward her sisters, face bright as morning sunshine. "Did I tell you that Lottie's been asked to be in the procession at the start of the junior rodeo?"

Zelda's heart squeezed, "I didn't know. That's precious."

Isobel washed down her cookie with a quick gulp of lemonade. "We're picking out a whole new outfit for her at the ranch gift shop. Lottie has made it clear. There must be fringe and sequins. And it absolutely must be pink."

Neve shifted a couple of hushpuppies to a napkin, her eyes twinkling with sisterly mischief as she focused on Zelda. "Do you think your new boyfriend gave her the part in the procession to suck up to you?"

"I think," Zelda said emphatically as she broke her own cookie into two halves, "that he gave her the honor because she's done a fabulous job with her riding lessons and he's a nice guy."

"Well," Neve retorted in her best schoolmarm voice, softened by a chuckle, "you sure put me in my place. Prickly, much?"

Shoulders stiffening, Zelda started to take offense... then realized her professor sister's grin was a bit too wide. Shifting on her wooden chair, she gently pushed

Neve's shoulder. "Did you say that on purpose to see if I would leap to his defense?"

"Why would I sink to subterfuge?" Neve pressed a hand to her chest in mock shock. "It's not like you're hiding anything from us. Are you?"

No need to keep pretending. Zelda shoved aside a stack of flyers and tugged closer her plate filled with a sandwich and hushpuppies, sagging back in her seat. "We are attracted to each other and apparently doing a poor job at hiding that from others. But it simply can't go anywhere."

Neve rested a gentle hand on her elbow. "Because you're still not over your breakup?"

That was the last thing she wanted to discuss. "Perhaps. And he's moving. We're better off as friends. Top Dog staff friends."

Isobel stacked the small bins on top of the clipboards and placed them all in a larger container. "Cash and I were friends for months before we came here," she said, her eyes taking on a dreamy look.

Zelda pressed a hand to her tightening heart again, reminded of how she and her sister hadn't stayed in touch these past few years. She needed to rectify that. "He was injured, right?"

"How have I not told you this?" Isobel sighed, then continued, "He was recovering from a firefighting work injury. And he went to the same rehabilitation center where Lottie received her occupational therapy. Well, anyway, we had simple conversations at first, moved on to having lunches together. Then dinners.

Accompanying each other to events like a concert in the park and a ball game."

Zelda couldn't resist asking, "When did you and Cash become more than friends?"

Isobel slumped back into her chair, her thumb stroking her glass along the condensation. "Lottie was celebrating her sixth birthday party with her friends at the center. Cash agreed to dress up like a pirate. One look at him making all those kids smile and something shifted inside me."

Neve clapped her hands together. "And you two lived happily ever after?"

"Well," Isobel snorted on a laugh. "I resisted for a while, of course. You know that my divorce was difficult... Anyway, when Gran's will gave us the mission to come here, Cash offered to help me drive from Montana. He still had a few weeks left until his return to work."

"That's so sweet."

Isobel scrunched her nose. "Truly. I'm deathly afraid of driving in the mountains so his help was invaluable."

"You? Afraid?" Zelda asked, surprised she didn't know this about her sibling. "You're one of the most fearless people I know." So many times in her life she wished she had her sister's grit, that she didn't have to pretend to be bold and daring. How wonderful would it be to have that come naturally?

Isobel's jaw trembled. "I'm absolutely terrified that we won't find a donor kidney in time for my daughter."

Eyes watering, Zelda angled forward to wrap her sister in the tightest of hugs, Neve following suit wrapping her arms around them both. For a moment, all their years apart, all the distance and unshared secrets melted away. They became the three siblings all but joined at the hip on adventures straight out of their grandmother's tales.

A knocking on the door broke the tenuous, resurrected bond. Zelda eased away back into her chair, scrubbing her wrist across her damp eyes. Neve's eyes were just as watery blue.

Clearing her throat, Isobel scraped back her chair. "Hold that thought. I'll only be a minute."

One ragged breath at a time, Zelda willed her emotions to calm so she and her sisters could finish their task and lunch. She needed to focus on her siblings and the task that brought them here. Finding Gran's long-lost son, which would hopefully lead them to a donor for Lottie. Nothing else could take precedence.

The front door creaked open and Isobel exclaimed, "Hello, Troy. Were your ears burning? Because we were just talking about you. What can I help you with?"

Zelda's heart stuttered as she clocked his presence in the doorway, awareness pinging through her.

Troy swept his Stetson off his head, his dark blond hair mussed and brushing his collar. "Is Zelda here? I really need to speak with her."

Neve chuckled behind her, muttering in a low, amused voice, "You're just friends, huh?"

Chapter Ten

Troy carried the crutches since Zelda insisted she could make her way from her sister's place back to her own cabin as long as she held on to the picket fence. Maisey trotted a few steps ahead like she owned the place all the way into Zelda's little front lawn. He allowed himself a moment to enjoy the look of her slim legs in jeans, the gentle sway of her hair along her spine. Troy wanted to scoop her up and carry her the rest of the way, but knew she would object.

Besides, he was on a mission to manage the misunderstanding with Levi. And that started with admitting to Zelda what had happened.

She hobbled to the porch, then sank down on a cushioned seat with a hefty sigh. "Whew. Before you know it, I'll be running marathons again. Well, if I ever ran them before."

He dropped to sit on a lower step and brought her foot to rest on his knee. "I'm sorry to take you away from your project. I know how important the donor drive is to your family—to Lottie."

"You have nothing to apologize for. We were just finishing up for the afternoon. We folded a hundred flyers, stuffed as many information packets, and addressed mail-outs to the press and local vendors. Isobel is going to finish up the online promo tonight."

"Sounds like you had a productive day." He held his Stetson in his hands, turning it round and round by the brim. "I truly am sorry to bother you, but I'm in a jam after that meeting with my investor."

"How so? Is there something I can do to help?"

His cheeks puffed with a long exhale. "Levi thinks we're dating."

"I'm sorry." Her hand flew to her chest, toying with her thin sliver chain, a tiny paw-print charm dangling. "I know you were hoping to avoid something like this happening."

"Actually, he's okay with it." Much to Troy's surprise and chagrin. "He thinks we make a nice couple. He was quite impressed with you."

She slid the silver charm back and forth. "I'm not quite sure what to say. I know that's got to put you in an awkward position."

"Here's the thing." He placed his hat to one side and rested his hands on her calf. He'd thought long and hard about the right approach on his way to see her. "No matter what I told him, he was locked in on his assessment of the situation. Would you mind terribly if we pretend to be a couple? Just until after the junior rodeo, when he leaves?"

Her pupils widened with awareness but she didn't draw her foot away. "It feels…deceitful."

"Because it is," he admitted, guilt kicking him like an unbroken mustang. He hated dragging her into a mess of his own making. "I'm just not sure how else to get around this, while protecting the deal for my daughter— Never mind. Forget I said anything. I'll figure something out."

Defeat weighed him down as he scrubbed a palm over his face.

"Hold on. Let's talk this through. What about Harper's feelings?" she asked, resting her hand on his arm as her attention swung back toward him. "And Lottie's, for that matter? I don't want either of them to get the wrong impression or have their feelings hurt when we have our inevitable 'breakup.'"

Heat he couldn't deny went through him at her touch. He leaned forward ever so slightly, drawn to her. Her vanilla scent mixed with the fragrance of the freshly cut grass in the little yard.

Maisey sneezed into the bed of flowers, stirring the delicate green leaves. The noise drew him back to the present.

He shook his head. "You're right. It's a bad idea and selfish of me to ask."

"Not selfish." angled forward to cup his face, blue eyes bright. "You're thinking of your daughter and that's admirable."

"Thanks for that." He appreciated the words more than he could say, needed them at a time he was feeling like he'd failed his kid. He leaned his cheek into her touch for a long moment until a bee buzzed past, causing them both to pull away.

She chewed her bottom lip, her forehead furrowed. "What if we tell Harper that we're trying to get the matchmakers to leave us alone? Because truth be told, back at the dream catcher workshop with all those romance stories and knowing looks, well, that felt mighty awkward. Wouldn't you agree?"

He couldn't argue with her on that point. "Most definitely."

"So it would help us *both* to avoid any more of that." She reached toward her dog as Maisey pranced over from the flowers and up the stairs, placing a paw on Zelda's leg.

He appreciated her letting him off the hook a bit with the emphasis on *both*. "And what about Lottie?"

She chewed her thumbnail for a moment before continuing, "We'll tell her that we are friends. That's not too far away from the truth, is it?"

"Zelda Dalton, you are a most likable person."

Staying silent, she smiled, her cheeks pink as she looked down at her pup. The scrunch of her nose and twinkle in her eyes warmed him.

He grinned in return. "That's your opening to say I'm not too bad."

The playful glimmer in her eyes multiplied as she looked up through lowered lashes. "You're not too bad."

Their laughter twined in the summer air, birds singing overhead and the wind whispering around them. Her chest rose and fell faster, a feeling he understood too well at the moment. He wanted to kiss her—thoroughly—but he also didn't want to upset the balance they found, the opportunity to see her without concocting excuses. Because yes, he couldn't deny that he looked forward to more time with her even if the circumstances were less than ideal. So he waited and let her take the lead.

Zelda nodded. "It's settled. We're officially a fake couple." She thrust out her hand. "Shake on it?"

He enfolded it with his and shook. And at the soft feel of her skin against his calloused fingertips, he knew that keeping his desire under control would be easier said than done. "Harper's taking her SAT tomorrow if you're free?"

Holding on to his hand, she let him help her to her feet again. "It's a date."

A date.

The two simple words had churned around in Zelda's mind all night long. Just fake dating, she reminded herself, to keep his focus—and hers—on making the junior rodeo a success for his sake and for her niece.

Not that downplaying the get-together had stopped Zelda from obsessing about her outfit. Certainly the glint in his eyes yesterday over her skirt and tank top had given her a thrill—and an ego boost. She shouldn't care what a man thought of her appearance. After all, healing her rattled self-esteem after her last relationship had been an important goal for her during her time at the ranch.

But Troy's appreciation still felt mighty darn good.

She smoothed her hands over her paisley silk skort, paired with a jean vest. Knee-high boots completed her ensemble, also giving her ankle extra support.

Her cell phone vibrated on the oak dining table, rattling and inching ever so slightly across. She snatched it up just before it knocked a dog-shaped saltshaker. "Hey there, Troy. What's up?"

Her voice sounded breathy even to her own ears. Could he be canceling?

"It went faster than I expected dropping off Harper for her SAT," he said. "Is this a good time, or should I come back later?"

His thoughtfulness tugged at her, stirring emotions she had meant to keep out of their relationship. She would have her hands full maintaining boundaries.

"Absolutely." Her pulse sped with relief. "All's quiet here. Isobel took Lottie into town for a doctor's appointment. Neve is giving a guest lecture online. Maisey is going to hang out at home today. She's been pretty busy lately for a senior pup."

"She sure doesn't act like a senior," he answered with a chuckle. "Glad you're ready. Because I'm outside."

"Oh," she said in surprise, straightening away from the table and looking around for her boho backpack. "I didn't hear your truck arrive."

"Because I'm not in the pickup."

Intrigued, she hobbled over to the window and parted the curtain and found... Troy waited out front sitting in an old-fashioned horse-drawn buckboard wagon.

The romanticism—and fun—of his gesture touched her. And she couldn't deny the extra beat to her heart at the sight of him in jeans and a gray T-shirt, the cotton stretched across his broad shoulders.

A stout gray Percheron horse swished its massive gray tail, sending a flurry of buzzing flies into the air. Troy's wide smile met her own as he adjusted his seat. His grip on the reins was loose and practiced, the leather tack gleaming in the sun.

She tugged open the front door and limped out to the porch. Shading her eyes with a hand, she called out, "Are you heading to the country store, farmer Troy?"

"I thought you might be going stir-crazy with those crutches. I know I would be. So I figured you might welcome an outside expedition."

With that one statement, he'd been more insightful than her ex in a year of living together. "I have to admit I'm growing weary with the extent of my fresh air coming from sitting on my porch."

"Or a picnic blanket," he said, referencing their time just after her injury.

She hoped she hadn't hurt his feelings or sounded ungrateful. She picked her way toward the gate, thankful to be moving under her own steam. "I had fun that evening. Thank you. But yes, the thought of moving around sounds amazing." She flexed her ankle a hint. "I'm almost ready to bear weight—and I can't wait. Pun intended."

"Well, meanwhile, I even have a cushion for you to prop your foot, if need be." He held up a throw pillow with a horseshoe print before leaping down from the bench.

Landing right beside her.

Her breath caught at his proximity.

"You're spoiling me." She gripped the side of the wagon, the rough wood abrasive against her fingertips.

"I've only just begun." He grasped her waist and lifted her up onto the buckboard. The seat offered a surprisingly high vantage point to see the world, like floating along the mountain.

Exciting.

All the more so for the man settling beside her, with his thigh pressed against hers. She cleared her throat, trying not to remember the feel of his hands on her waist. "What did you tell Harper about our, uh, arrangement?"

"As we planned, I just told her we would be spending more time together to stop people from trying to set us up with others."

"And she said?"

"She said something like 'fine, cool' and went off to her room with a pile of pizza." He shrugged, cheeks puffing with a sigh. "Thanks for the SAT prep sites you sent to Harper. That was thoughtful."

"She's an amazing kid." Zelda leaned into the summer breeze carrying a wildflower scent. She nudged his shoulder. "Two days ago, a young family dropped off their golden retriever puppy. The little girl—she was maybe five or six—had been crying. She was afraid to leave her dog behind. Harper sat on the ground with her, asked what the puppy's favorite treats were and just made the precious imp feel a lot better. Then she gave her a paw-print friendship bracelet and said they were 'best friends now and best friends made sure that puppies were taken care of always.' The child stopped crying and gave her a hug."

The hopeful look in Troy's eyes tugged at her as he silently took in her words. He adjusted his hold on the reins as they drove past a wedding party standing under twinkle lights strung from the trees. The men wore Stetsons and boleros, with starched white shirts and jeans. The bridesmaids wore pale pink, knee-length dresses with buff boots. Raise the Woof provided live music as the bride processioned.

Troy's tanned face showed the edges of a smile at the story. She loved that easy look resting on his lips. "Your daughter also volunteered to revise the appointment scheduling survey. She's a natural at organization and logic. I was impressed."

Shifting the leather reins to one hand, Troy laced his fingers with hers, giving a quick squeeze that sent butterflies to every part of her body before he let go. "I think you are a good influence on her."

With her other hand, she gripped the edge of her seat as they jostled along the path—and also to steady her quivering insides. "I've only been here a couple of months, but this is by far the most magical place on earth."

She knew the legend of Sulis Cave and the reputed healing properties of the spring's water. More and more, she found herself believing in the goodness of the land, of this place. The love at Top Dog Dude Ranch was hard to deny. Staff and guests alike waved as they passed by. She reveled in the simple joy of recognition, community, the anchoring heartbeat of seeing and being seen. It felt like a royal tour—ranch style.

Troy adjusted his Stetson with a knuckle nudge. "I've been to a lot of dude ranches, and this place is definitely one of a kind. I hope some of their magic rubs off as I launch my facility."

Laughter and cheers drifted from the valley, drawing her gaze toward the recent expansion for guests who preferred a glamping experience. The vintage restored campers were nestled in between trees, the pastel pinks, blues and teals giving a callback to gentler, long-ago times. A few yards away, a private cove came stocked with canoes and paddleboats. The shoreline sported picnic tables and a massive stone firepit.

"Gran told us all sorts of stories set in a place so much like this," Zelda said, "but she also seemed to have a sense for when one of us needed a tale specialized for just one sister. She wove a whole series about a quirky little girl who climbed trees in the magical forest."

"It tracks with those fairy-tale names you and your sisters have."

Sun warming the leather, she adjusted in her seat. "Perhaps a little hokey."

"But a nice way for your parents to honor your grandmother's storytelling tradition."

She was touched that he remembered what she'd said, something that settled inside her like a breath of fresh mountain air.

They continued in companionable silence, the kind that came from knowing someone well. When had they shifted into that stage? But there was no denying the transition.

The wagon rumbled past the lengthy greenhouse. A group of children sat on blankets weaving floral crowns and necklaces. She loved so much about this place, not the least of which the way the ranch opened its doors to four-legged critters. Guests walked their dogs along the trails—including a golden retriever who looked a lot like her grooming client Comet.

Zelda rested a hand on Troy's knee. "Thank you for my dream catcher. I've hung it in my kitchen window."

"What dreams do you have, Zelda Dalton?"

"Hmm… That my niece gets her kidney match soon. Other than that, I have everything I want living and working here."

He looked at her hand, but before she could move it, he rested his on top of hers. Butterflies stirred inside her, not unlike the monarchs sipping on honeysuckle. But she needed to be wary that bees also lurked and she was too vulnerable to having her emotions stung again.

She bit her bottom lip. "I hate to end this wonderful afternoon, but I promised Lottie that after she gets back from her appointment, I would take her to a pack-tivity while her mother writes."

"Is it something I would enjoy?" He winked. "In the interest of future dates."

"I doubt it's your style." Her hand twitched along his knee, gripping firmer. "We're going to the ice cream shop for a taffy-pulling party. I'll be sure to bring you a sample."

His deep brown eyes held hers for so long she wondered what churned inside that handsome head of his. But she was content to wait, enjoying the view, taking in the rugged planes of his tanned face, the soap-fresh scent of him filling each breath.

Even though there was no one watching them to take note of the fake date, he rubbed his thumb along her wrist and asked, "How would you feel about me giving you both a ride home later in a buggy? Would Isobel approve?"

She moistened her damp lips, swallowing to clear the tightening in her throat. "I'll check to be sure, but I'm certain my sister will be thrilled—as will Lottie."

And Zelda couldn't lie to herself. She was already counting down the hours.

Troy waited outside the Bone Appetit Barkery shop with Lottie sitting next to him while Zelda spoke to a client inside. He'd switched out the rugged buckboard wagon for a surrey-style buggy—complete with fringe on top—with cushioned benches that had better seating for Lottie.

He had to admit, the fake dating with Zelda was working out better than he'd expected. He'd actually had fun today. He was glad Zelda had agreed to extending the day.

The adorable six-year-old sat beside him, wearing jean shorts, a red plaid shirt and a matching hair bow. His friends on the rodeo circuit had laughed at him more than once as he fixed his daughter's hair when she was little. But he prided himself on being a good girl-dad.

Cocoa, the child's service dog, lay on the buggy floor at her feet, a chocolate Labrador retriever with a red plaid bow on her collar, too. If it weren't for the Lab's service dog vest and the braces on Lottie's legs, it would be easy to forget the challenges the little girl faced from spina bifida.

Lottie chewed and chewed, her cheeks puffed with two pieces of saltwater taffy. Finally, she swallowed with an exaggerated gulp and said, "Mr. Troy, I brought you some taffy, and some for Harper, too. It's in my bag. But here's a piece to taste now." She passed over a fat glob wrapped in wax paper, ends twisted. "It's a licorice one. They're not my favorite. Is that a bad thing for me to say?"

He shifted toward her, head bowing slightly in the enclosed black buggy. She plopped the taffy into his hand with a satisfied grin.

"Not at all. It's very sweet of you to share your treats and I love licorice flavor." He adjusted the reins in his left hand and the Percheron let out a low nicker, head tossing. "Are you sure you want to give some away?"

She bobbed her head in an emphatic yes as her fingers drummed on the leather seat. "I have plenty for me and my mommy and Cash. And Aunt Zelda said she'll bring me back to shop for more. They sell it. And ice cream, too—some for people and some for dogs."

"Then I'll just say thank you very much and I can't wait another minute to sample a piece." He untwisted the waxed paper around a pink glob and popped it in his mouth, chewing, and chewing…and chewing. The sugary flavor melted along his taste buds.

Glancing back to the Bone Appetit Barkery, he tracked Zelda's movements through the glass, the glossy sway of her ponytail. She threw her head back in laughter as she moved from the left side of the store where human sweets were sold to the right side where dog-friendly baked goods lined cases. He swallowed the last bit of the taffy before letting out a sigh of contentment. "Really good. I'll have to sign up for the next party at the Bone Appetit."

Lottie looked at him with wide, serious eyes. Moments before, a smile had rested easy on her face. Now the child's face went slack, worry knitting her brow. "I don't know if I'll be able to go. I'm waiting on my surgery."

His throat tightened with emotion and a sense of urgency to find the help this child needed. He struggled for what to say, not wanting to mention something wrong or upsetting. He settled for a simple, logical reply. "I'll make extra, then, when it's my turn and I'll share with you, like you shared with me."

"Okay…" She chewed her bottom lip for a moment. "I gotta get a new kidney. When we find one. So don't know when that's gonna be." Her chin quivered a bit. Cocoa sat up and rested her head on the girl's knee and Lottie began stroking her pup. "I feel sad that somebody has to get surgery for me to get better."

His heart split open a bit at her words. What a heavy weight for a small child to carry. He wouldn't have minded petting the dog, too, but he knew he wasn't allowed to distract Cocoa while she worked.

He schooled his face to remain calm, unwilling to

add to Lottie's worries. "What does your mom say about that?"

"I haven't told her." She stroked Cocoa's head faster, rhythmically. The dog scooted closer to her young ward, gently pressing against her legs. "I don't want her to be scared. And she'll just say it's okay. That the person wants to help me."

All fair answers, and Troy wasn't sure he could do any better in Isobel's shoes. This was a journey no parent—or child—should have to face. He did know that Lottie wanted and needed more from him in this moment, so he searched for the safest thing to say to bide time until he could hand over the child to her mother.

"You know what I think? I believe people who get tested already know what an honor it is to help someone else. I wish I could be that person for you, kiddo." He glanced back toward Zelda at the threshold of the glass door flecked with cling-on paw prints.

"Have you had surgery?" Lottie peered up at him with inquisitive eyes.

Now that he could answer easily. He pushed up the sleeve on his T-shirt to show a long scar that started on his shoulder. "This one's from when I got thrown by a bull and broke my collarbone. And I've got another on my shin from when I broke my leg." No need to tell her a horse kicked him that time. "And couple more where I just got stitches."

She touched his shoulder lightly, carefully. "Did it hurt?"

His heart broke the rest of the way. "I won't lie to

you. It did hurt, but the doctor gave me medicine so I slept when they fixed it and that helped a lot."

Her forehead furrowed as she seemed to mull over his answer. And as he watched her process information that would strain even an adult's understanding, he knew that just as he would move heaven and earth for his daughter, he also had to do everything humanly possible to help this child.

And that included watching his step with the girl's aunt.

Chapter Eleven

Zelda wondered what had turned Troy's spirit so somber since he'd arrived at the café to pick her up along with Lottie. When he'd arrived in the adorable surrey, he'd been all smiles, in the best of moods. But on the drive back to take Lottie home, he'd been silent, leaving her niece to jabber about her exciting day while sharing pieces of fresh pulled taffy.

But Zelda knew she couldn't ask him just yet, not as they stopped outside Isobel's cabin with Cash waiting in a candy-apple-red Adirondack chair, whittling. The burly former firefighter pushed to his feet and lumbered over. He showed little sign of the injury on the job that had led to his early retirement. Now he worked at the ranch in the stables. He was a good guy. Zelda had enjoyed getting to know him.

She placed a hand over her brow to block out the intense midday summer sun streaming through the open-air windows as Cash approached the buggy.

"Thank you for bringing our girls home," Cash said, passing a whittled dog toy to Lottie, who squealed in excitement as she clutched the gift to her chest.

Troy nodded. "My pleasure. I'm glad to chauffeur this little princess anytime."

"Cash, thank you for my present," Lottie said, extending her arms for him to sweep her from the front seat effortlessly. Cocoa soared from the surrey and to the ground.

Isobel walked out onto the front porch, meeting the dog at the bottom of the steps. Sunlight filtered through clusters of nearby sycamores and oaks, dancing over Isobel's red maxi dress, making her seem a bit like a glittering fairy from one of their grandmother's stories. She knelt and removed the dog's vest. "Cocoa's had a full day so she's due some playtime, too."

Isobel joined Cash as he settled Lottie on a quilt, anchored to the ground by a picnic basket. They made such a sweet-looking family, the three of them. Zelda was happy for them. After her sister's divorce, she deserved happiness, peace. Love.

Zelda just wished her own path to healing after her breakup could be as smooth.

Her stomach clenched at the echoes of that pain, and she pressed her palm into the leather seat of the buggy.

Her sister, Cash and Lottie waved their goodbyes as a monarch butterfly flitted around under the buggy's canopy before escaping toward the sky. Clicking his tongue softly, Troy prompted the Percheron to action. The draft horse moved forward, ambling toward Zelda's cottage.

Steady hoof falls thudded against the dirt road. As the silence stretched, she debated trying to draw Troy out, to find out what had caused the shift in his mood.

But finally he spoke. "In my work with horses, I understand the role of equine therapy with horses helping multiple people. And I get how that same principle can work with therapy dogs helping in a clinic setting." He cast a quick glance her way before returning his attention to the road. "But I don't know a lot about service dogs, beyond the general idea of a stranger not touching them or interrupting their tasks."

Beneath her, the buggy's wheels groaned to a halt in front of her cottage. Overhead, a large fluffy white cloud rolled past the sun, throwing dark shadows across the lush green grass of her tiny yard.

Zelda picked at the end of her dark braid absently. "I'm only just learning more from my sister, but those two points are definitely crucial. The way my sister has explained it to me, therapy dogs work with a group and a service dog is for one individual who has a disability."

"Ah," he said with a pensive nod, the light catching on the handsome angles of his face. "That makes sense as to why the dog focusing on the person is so important."

Could this have something to do with his shift in mood? She was curious enough to stay in the surrey and let the conversation play out. "Cocoa is a mobility dog, assisting Lottie with things like shifting in and out of her wheelchair. Pulling up the covers at night. Tugging socks on. She also performs tasks to help when Lottie is suffering from neuropathy pain—Cocoa presses, using counter pressure to alleviate the discomfort. Overall, Cocoa knows more than seventy cues."

"No kidding?" His eyebrows lifted in surprise mingled with admiration. "And Lottie knows all of these, too?"

"She can cue them all, yes, but many times, Cocoa senses the need before Lottie or her mom are aware." Zelda toyed with a bit of wax paper left over from a piece of taffy. "I use the word *cue* rather than *command* because theirs is a partnership."

Grabbing the brace for the canopy, Zelda eased herself from the buggy, careful to test her balance with her sore ankle, then starting toward her cabin. Trying not to focus on the heat that flooded neck to cheek, she swallowed as they continued toward the cottage porch.

"That makes sense." His hand braced her back as they moved toward the stairs. "I think Cocoa was comforting Lottie while we were waiting for you to come out from the café."

Comforting? She glanced over her shoulder at him following her up the walkway. "What happened?"

Their little cove felt utterly private, with only a hint of voices carrying on the wind. The music of birds talking back and forth between trees mixed with the light percussion of rustling branches. A stream rippled in the distance.

He dipped his head closer. "Lottie talked about needing a new kidney and how she feared it might hurt—because she was worried about the donor hurting while helping her."

Her hand flew to her mouth. "Oh no, that poor kid. What did you say to her?"

"I tried to keep the answer simple, that it hurts but

gets better." His forehead pinched with worry. "She also wanted to see my scars from rodeo injuries."

"That definitely sounds like Lottie," Zelda said, affection swelling inside her. "She's something else."

Zelda limped up the steps, each plank creaking a weathered hello as she made her way to the door. A new sunflower wreath, probably a gift from Neve, now stood watch on the wooden cottage door. She stroked the petals before punching in the security code. With a pleasant chirp, the door unlocked as her pup gave an excited yip. Maisey darted through the door, sailing down the steps and running to her favorite corner of the picket fence.

Pivoting to face him, Zelda leaned against a porch post, unable to resist asking with a teasing tone, "So where are those scars?"

Troy threw back his head, a laugh rumbling free. The strong column of his neck called to her, making her ache to press a kiss right over where his pulse throbbed. It had been so long since she'd felt this ramp of desire, since she had felt it directed toward her as well.

As Troy's laugh faded, his gaze met hers, his brown eyes turning molten black. She swayed toward him and his hand cupped her waist, drawing her closer. He skimmed his mouth across hers once, twice, holding. Her lips parted in a sigh and invitation that he answered with a low growl of desire. He slid his arms around her, her breasts pressing against the hard wall of his chest.

She started to back him toward the door, not sure

how far they would take this, but certain things were moving beyond anything that should happen out in public. She reached behind her for the doorknob just as—

Maisey yelped from the yard.

And yelped again, with a high-pitched, repetitive squeal of pain.

Troy pulled away and shot down the steps ahead of her. She made fast tracks after him, disregarding any twinges in her ankle. Worry for her pup fueled her.

Kneeling, Toy cradled Maisey in his broad and gentle hands, checking her over and muttering soft, soothing words. "What's the matter, girl? Where does it hurt?"

All too quickly, the answer became apparent as a bright red spot on the dog's nose began swelling. An angry wasp swept by and away.

Zelda scooped her dog from his hands carefully, cradling her close. "Oh no, looks like she got stung by a wasp on her nose."

Troy braced a palm on her spine as they rushed back up the steps, footsteps thudding on the wooden planks. "That can be dangerous if the swelling closes off her airway."

"I'm going to give her an antihistamine right away." She shouldered through the front door. On instinct, she flipped the light switch on her way into the cottage, darting as best she could for the decorative bin of medicine sitting on the built-in wooden bookshelf that flanked the fireplace. "I just need to look up the safe dosage for her weight."

"What if she needs to go to the veterinarian?" He strode to the freezer and pulled out ice cubes, wrapping them in a couple of paper towels.

"I can drive if I need to. Or call one of my sisters." She passed Maisey over to him. "Can you hold her and ice her nose while I look for the antihistamine?"

"Of course." He took Maisey back and sat on the emerald green sofa, carefully touching the ice to her swollen nose. "I'll stay however long you need."

Zelda pivoted with the medicine bag in her hand. "What about Harper?"

"I'll talk to her." His voice rumbled with a calm assurance and strength, quieting Maisey.

"Thank you." Swallowing down tears, she drew in a shaky breath, not wanting to dwell overlong on how good it felt to lean on him.

Troy leaned on the porch post, cell phone in hand as he called his daughter. He hoped he wasn't making a mistake in trusting her to be alone for a few hours, but he also couldn't track her 24/7 indefinitely.

He and Zelda had been running from the attraction for the past two months. While he waited to see if Zelda would need a ride to the veterinarian seemed as good a time as any to face the attraction and decide what step to take next.

At least that was the rationale he was telling himself for why he needed to stay. The memory of that kiss they'd shared was definitely chasing around in his thoughts, too.

"Hey, Harper, I'm hung up here at Zelda's." He

scuffed the toe of his boot on the porch, squinting as his gaze lingered on the flower bed filled with butter-flies. "Maisey got stung on the nose by a wasp and the swelling is pretty bad. I'm hanging out until we see if Zelda needs a ride to the veterinarian."

"Poor Maisey," Harper said, with genuine sympathy in her voice. No doubt, his daughter loved that pup. "That really sucks."

He stared past the trio of Dalton cabins toward his own. "What are you doing?"

"I'm on the sofa with my laptop." In the distance, the living room curtains fluttered through the open window. "I'm hitting the send key as we speak. I just finished my homework assignment on *Wuthering Heights*."

"That's really great. I'm proud of the way you're applying yourself." He hoped he hadn't pushed too hard, though. She deserved time to be a kid. "Although it would have been okay if you took some time off after all the SAT prep and testing."

"Thanks, but I'm glad to have it done. And, well," she said in a tone that relayed an ulterior motive, "I was hoping to get in your good graces so I could go to the zip-lining. There's a group of teens signed up for the class, and yes, before you ask, Wynn is planning to go."

Ah. Now they were getting to the heart of the matter. He weighed what to say and came up with a question to buy himself more time to think.

"Who's chaperoning?"

"Really?" Her voice squeaked with surprise. "You're considering it?"

"Who's chaperoning?" he asked again. His gaze stayed fixed on their cabin as birdsong filled the air around him.

"Mrs. Susanna—she's the librarian." Harper's words tumbled on top of each other with excitement. "And her husband, Mr. Micah, will be there, too. He's the contractor guy. Oh, and Mr. Gil is the instructor for the event. Do you want me to text you their numbers so you can check?"

He hated the suspicion creeping through that she might have a friend on the other end of that number. But he also didn't want to accuse her without cause. So he settled for a neutral answer. "I've got their numbers on my employee roster."

He waited for her to panic, if she'd been fibbing.

"Cool, Dad," she said, sounding like her old self. "Thanks."

He breathed a sigh of relief, sticking a thumb through the belt loop of his faded jeans. "Have fun, and come straight home afterward, okay?"

"Yep, got it." She paused without disconnecting, then said, "I won't let you down."

"Love you, Harper."

She chuckled. Her real laugh. A sound he hadn't heard in what felt like years. "Yeah, yeah, don't go getting all sappy on me."

He ended the call with more hope than he'd felt in a long time. Finally, he was making progress and thankfully he had extra eyes to help him ensure his daughter's safety.

After sending quick texts to Gil and to Micah—the

confirmations and assurances swooping in fast—he straightened and went back inside the cabin. Pausing in the threshold as his eyes adjusted to the soft, dim lights, his breath caught. Zelda's delicate face down-turned, wisps of her dark hair cascading, wavy from being released from its normal braid. Cross-legged on the dark green sofa, she cooed to Maisey. The little white fluffball gazed lovingly at Zelda as she panted.

She looked up, swooping her hair back over her shoulder. "Everything okay with Harper? I don't want to keep you from her."

"All's good. She's going zip-lining with some other kids. Susanna and Micah are chaperoning. I'm just finishing up texting them to confirm this little outing is on the up-and-up. And for them to make sure she shows on time and doesn't leave early."

"I did read about the event, so that much is true." She stroked Maisey's back. "I think Neve was going, too. I'll message her if you wish."

"That would be great." He tapped his temple. "Just for my peace of mind. Thanks."

"Of course." Her fingers flew across her cell phone's keyboard. A message swooped in just as fast. "She's on it. She says she'll ask them to join her group for supper tonight and will send photos throughout."

He breathed a sigh of relief as he sank into the cushion next to her, adjusting to better angle toward her. "I can't tell you how much I appreciate the help."

"Were your parents strict?"

"Not particularly. I was a late-in-life baby and I suspect they never planned," *or wanted,* "to have kids. As long as I did my schoolwork and didn't rock the boat, I was free to do as I wished." Was he overcompensating for that lack by being hypervigilant about his daughter?

"I'm sorry." She leaned her shoulder against his in a gentle comfort, with an ease that showed a shift in their relationship.

Her vanilla scent teased him, making his heart race.

For a moment, he considered kissing her again, but as quickly discarded the notion. He didn't want to press her, to risk losing her trust. And Maisey was also counting on them to keep watch over her puffy red nose.

He rested his hand on top of Zelda's for an instant before taking the soggy paper towels from her. "How about I make a more durable ice pack and then rustle us up something to eat?"

Harper tipped her face into the late afternoon mountain breeze whispering through the trees, like an echo of the wind she'd felt when she'd zip-lined. Wynn said she'd been fearless. She just knew that being able to shout until her lungs darn near burst had felt good. Really good. Like she'd finally gotten to pour out all the anger inside her.

She'd zip-lined three more times until she'd been emptied. Above the oak and sycamores, harness hugging her body, Harper had flung an arm out. Wind whipped across her in a sensation of flying. She felt at home, eyes taking in the dark greens of trees, ravines and glittering rivers below, the low hum of the others around her fading for a moment. She didn't want the day to end.

Shaking her head clear so she could pay attention, she unbuckled her harness and listened to the adventure leader wrap up the session.

Gil stood with his feet braced on the rocky outcropping, the valley and zip line behind him. "I hope everyone enjoyed today's expedition. Be sure to check the Top Dog app that you downloaded at check-in for more Adventures with Gil."

She stepped out of the harness, bracing a hand on an oak tree trunk for balance. Then, she hoisted the harness over her shoulder. "Hey, Neve," she said softly. "It's so cool that you get to do all this kind of nature watching for your job."

Neve laughed, adjusting her cap over her perfect long hair that hadn't gotten in the least messy. "Well, if you ever want to hear more about becoming a wildlife biologist, I'll be happy to fill you in. Although truth be told, most of it is far more sedate."

"I'll keep that in mind." Harper knelt to retie her left sneaker. "Thanks for helping me get the hang of it."

Neve lowered her voice, giving Harper a shoulder nudge. "That fellow over there seemed like he would have been more than happy to assist you."

Harper laughed, eyeing Wynn, who was talking to another teen boy. He had a sixth sense or something because he looked over his shoulder, catching Harper's eye, a toothy grin spreading across his face. He tipped his Stetson at her.

Swoon. "I didn't want to look silly in front of him."

"Well, honey, I can sure understand that." Neve angled to whisper, "Go on back over and talk to him again before that lovelorn-puppy expression breaks everyone's heart."

Sneakers shifting the gravel beneath her stride, Harper wove through the crowd of ten like-minded adventurous teens. A tall sixteen-year-old blond gave her a high five as she passed by. The last few months, she hadn't felt much like being around anyone, until meeting Wynn, of course. But today as she moved through the forest floor amid old trees and the sounds of summer birds, she had to admit it was nice to be out doing something as a group. She collected one more high five as she stopped next to Wynn.

He linked his fingers with her lightly. "I'm glad you could come today. I wasn't sure you would be able to make it."

"I still can't believe my dad agreed." Her breath hitched in her chest at the feel of holding Wynn's hand, of not having to hide. His touch made her feel safe. "Although he checked with the chaperones." She touched her chest, wincing. "So embarrassing."

"He worries." Wynn squeezed her hand, his forehead furrowing. "That's what parents are supposed to do."

Her stomach clenched a little at the judgy sound in his voice. Shaking her head, she stared at her scuffed sneakers. "He probably just wanted to make sure how long I would be out of the way so he could hang out with Zelda."

As she said it, she felt foolish for believing his story

about needing to stay because of Maisey and a little old wasp sting. She hadn't paid much attention when he'd told her they decided to fake date in order to stifle the would-be matchmakers. But was that just a cover story, too?

Wynn dipped his head to catch her eye. "I thought you said he might have to drive Zelda and Maisey to the veterinarian."

"Sure," she said, dropping his hand. She crossed her arms over her chest. "Whatever."

His smile faded. "Your dad's single, though. And so is she. So what if they do decide to date?"

A little bolt of panic shot through her as she really weighed the idea.

"It matters because my mom's coming back," she insisted, her chin jutting.

"Okay, okay." He raised both of his hands in surrender. "Whatever you say. All I meant was that your dad deserves a life, too."

Tipping back her head, Harper blinked away the stupid tears welling in her eyes. Just from the wind blowing, though.

Neve waved for her attention. "Hey, you two. We're heading over to supper now and we've made sure there's a table for the whole group. Wanna join in?" Neve leaned in. "I've already cleared it with your dad when I messaged my sister."

Wynn's cheer filled her ears and she managed to rouse up an answering echo in return. Because even as she packed her gear from the day's zip-lining and returned it to the wagon, all the bad feelings she'd poured out were stacking back up again inside her.

This wasn't home, and she didn't belong here. She didn't belong anywhere, really.

She couldn't escape the sense that she didn't deserve happiness. Even her own mother hadn't wanted to stick around. Her dad was just doing the right thing by taking care of her. Wynn probably liked her because she was the only teenage girl staying at the ranch for the whole summer.

So even as she joined their group heading to supper, she knew that all this "happiness" was too good to last.

Chapter Twelve

Country music played softly over her phone as Zelda watched Troy pull containers from the cabinets to store the remnants of the supper scattered along the kitchen island. Troy had placed a delivery order from the ranch's little grocery store, surprising her with grilled hamburgers and fresh ears of corn. He'd even made potato wedges, crisped with olive oil and rosemary.

She'd been surprised—and charmed—by his culinary efforts. And deeply thankful for his support while she watched her recovering pet. Zelda shuffled Maisey to the overstuffed plaid dog bed on the sofa to monitor the swelling and her pup's respiration. She rested her hand along the pup's rib cage, taking comfort in the steady rise and fall, a mesmerizing rhythm that relaxed her back into the cushions, allowing herself the indulgence of staring at Troy. An urge she'd fought for the past two months.

A memory of those early days swept over her, reminding her of how the sight of him had drawn her from the start…

Zelda had really, really intended to go to the potpourri-making workshop. But she'd had to walk by the stables. Next thing she knew, her feet were detouring into the small arena.

Both wide doors were open invitingly, after all.

The cheers of the spectators drifted along the summer breeze, all the more enticement to check out Troy Shaw's lasso demo. She didn't venture all the way inside, instead lingering in the gaping opening. Half in. Half out. A noncommittal stance. She leaned against the frame, likely not even noticeable as she watched.

No question about it, he owned the ring as he went through his moves on horseback and off. He sailed the rope through the air, creating shapes and aerial maneuvers that defied gravity. Half the time, he wasn't even looking at the loop, rather entertaining the crowd with his commentary.

And all without ever once losing his Stetson. His broad shoulders stretched the plaid shirt. But then she'd drooled over those shoulders more than once. Today her gaze was drawn to his lean hips in denim and chaps.

Beyond his good looks and hot body, the man had charisma in spades. The mere sight of him sent tingles through her, the kind she hadn't felt in far too long. Thank goodness he was arrogant so it was easier to resist him. That didn't mean, though, she couldn't keep watching him from a distance. For his entire show, mesmerizing her so that her feet stayed planted even through the stable manager—Eliza—showing off her barrel racing skills on her quarter horse, Cricket. Eliza and the sleek brown animal moved as one to the delight of the onlookers.

"Hello there," Troy's deep voice rumbled over Zelda's shoulder.

She spun on her sneaker heel, surprised she'd been so dazed she hadn't even noticed him make his way outside. He must have circled around.

Not that it mattered how he'd gotten here. In front of her. Wide-shouldered and better-looking than any human had a right to be.

The more important question? How long had she been standing here gawking at him? She swallowed down the lump in her throat and willed her hormones to simmer down. "Great show. Everyone seemed to really enjoy themselves."

Cheers and applause still rumbled from inside, although the grounds outside were nearly deserted. Just her. The cowboy. And a few grazing horses in the pasture minding their own business.

"Thanks, Miss Zelda. But they were an easy crowd to impress," he drawled before looking back over her shoulder. "Where's your niece? I didn't see her come here with you."

So he'd noticed her watching him. Zelda's heart lurched. "Lottie's at a music workshop being led by Raise the Woof over in one of the other barns."

"Sounds fun." He leaned back against the planked outdoor wall of the arena. "They're a talented bunch."

Zelda basked in the sound of his bourbon-rich voice, all the while knowing she should go. Should. And she would. Soon. "I hope they're prepared. Lottie's a bit tone-deaf."

His lopsided smile pushed a dimple into his weathered, tanned cheek. "Then I'm sure they'll have plenty of percussion instruments on hand."

A faint hint of music carried on the wind along with the distant whinny of horses and the bleating of goats from the petting zoo.

When Troy didn't make a move to leave, she nodded toward the arena where Eliza was sparring with the rodeo clown. "I'm surprised to see her—the stable manager—here. I thought Eliza was in the band. But then I've met so many new people the past couple of weeks, I could be mixing them up."

Such a simple conversation, but easy somehow, and so very different from their prickly past encounters.

"The band actually has a flexible number of members. Some positions are even doubled up. That way everyone in the group doesn't have to miss work for an event—it makes scheduling easier." As he leaned back, Troy braced one boot on the wall, his dusty chaps making her fingers itch to test the texture. His big rodeo champ belt buckle gleamed in the afternoon sun. "The band has even tapped me to join in on occasion over the summer."

Was there anything this man couldn't do? When they were handing out attributes in heaven, he'd stood in more than his fair share of lines.

"What do you play?" she asked, half expecting him to rattle off half an orchestra's worth of instruments.

"The harmonica." His grin broadened, his eyes sheepish as if embarrassed for some reason.

There was a story in there somewhere. She was sure. And curious to know someday.

"A man of many talents." Not what she'd expected, but it fit his whole sexy-cowboy vibe. A vibe she would be wise to resist. "Well, I should let you get back to your adoring fans."

Troy clasped her arm lightly to stop her. "Do you have a minute more?"

"Uh, sure," she agreed, her voice far too breathy for her peace of mind. But after ogling him for the last half hour, his touch left her all the more unsteady.

"Thanks," he said, releasing her arm, his hand trailing away. Clearing his throat, he hooked his thumbs in his belt loops, his weathered face taking on that sheepish air again. "I owe you an apology. I'm sorry for being brusque, cutting you off the other day when my daughter came by."

Okay, but she didn't remember him being abrupt at all. She recalled hightailing it out of there, unsettled by the attraction to him. Not that she intended to admit as much.

So, instead she opted for a benign answer. "Her name is Harper, right?"

"Yeah." Nodding, he studied his dusty boots with undue attention. "She's having a tough time since her mom walked out on us."

Even as she willed herself not to feel sorry for him, her heart squeezed in sympathy for his daughter. "That's rough. I'm sorry—for both of you."

"I'm focused on getting her leveled out." His gaze rose again, meeting hers full-on, steely and determined.

She blinked fast. Had he thought she was hitting

on him? Her cheeks heated with embarrassment. "Of course you are. As a father should be."

"Let me clarify." He scratched along his collarbone. "I just don't want you to take it personally that I wasn't returning your interest."

The heat of embarrassment morphed to outright anger. "My what?"

To think she'd almost felt sorry for him long enough to forget his arrogance. She perched her hands on her hips and stood nose to nose with him. Well, almost, since she had to look up so far.

"Uh, pardon me if I misread things." He held up his hands defensively, his palms strong and calloused and very close to her shoulders. "It just seems you've been showing up with your niece quite often, and then today without her. I need to be clear I'm not..."

"Not what?" she asked tightly, mighty close to stomping off. Only curiosity held her still a moment longer.

His sigh was long and heavy, caressing her cheeks with a phantom kiss. "I'm making a mess of things."

"That's an understatement." Her pride was still stinging and she searched for a way to turn this around. To save face. And walk away with her dignity in place. "In fact, the reason I came here today was to tell you people are gossiping about the two of us. And we need to put a stop to it."

There. That made for a decent, face-saving cover story since it was true that people were talking, even if that wasn't her reason for hanging out at the arena like some buckle bunny.

His mouth went tight. *"I couldn't agree with you more. The last thing I need is gossip that I'm hooking up with a Top Dog staff member."*

Alrighty, then. And that was about all her pride could take for one day. Without a word, she spun away, ready to make fast tracks to anywhere else on this ranch. Except no more than two steps later, she stepped into a gopher hole. Her arms flailed as she began falling forward.

"Careful there," Troy cautioned, fast on his feet to catch her.

"I'm fine," she bit out, scrambling to find her footing without much success.

Then his strong arms shot out to loop around her waist, hefting her up as if she weighed less than nothing. She leaned back into the hard-muscled wall of his chest. The scent of leather and sweat seeped into her every breath as he eased her to her feet and turned her to face him.

She grabbed his shoulders, steadying herself as they stood chest to chest. The warmth of him radiated through her work shirt, launching a fresh wash of heat through her veins. Was it her imagination or had his heart rate kicked up a notch? Hers sure had.

His eyes were the most beautiful shade of amber. She hadn't noticed that before and now she couldn't look away. His hands clenched tighter around her arms. She wasn't sure who moved closer first, but his mouth was brushing hers. Ever so slightly and ever so intense at the same time.

Too much so for such a simple kiss.

Her heart hammering, Zelda tore herself away from him, holding up a hand to forestall any words from his arrogant mouth. With all the dignity she could muster, she strode past him toward the lodge—far away from Troy Shaw—her co-worker for the rest of the summer...

And even as the memory faded, she couldn't escape the notion that somehow, here she was again, craving the chance to spend time with him.

Sitting on the sofa as he sealed up the last of the leftovers, Zelda rubbed a tiny paw pensively. "She's breathing better now, don't you think?"

"Absolutely, especially compared to two hours ago when it happened." He slid the plastic containers filled with leftovers into the refrigerator, then nudged the door closed with his boot. "The swelling's gone down, too. Those antihistamines are also helping her snooze right through the discomfort."

Tears blurred her sight and she scrubbed her wrist over her eyes. A sigh rocked her body, giving temporary ease. "Sorry to go all weepy on you. I'm just so relieved."

"I can tell how much she means to you." Troy grabbed up their two stoneware plates, scraping the bits of food into her stainless steel trash can with a fork.

"She was my companion through the darkest time of my life." She looked up self-consciously, realizing exactly why she was so attached to her dog. Now more than ever. "Right before my breakup, then afterward, too."

"Heartbreak is rough," he said, holding her gaze

while placing the dinner plates and cooking utensils in the dishwasher, "even with the best of buddies to comfort you."

"I don't mean to be overly dramatic." She pressed a hand to her tightening rib cage, watching him as he sprayed down the countertops with lemon-scented cleaner. Somehow it seemed easier to share the pain of her past when he wasn't looking at her. "It was more than heartbreak. My ex was, well, *controlling* would be an understatement. It took everything inside me to break free and relocate here."

His eyes met hers across the room, his focus shifting entirely. She felt rattled inside. She'd never shared the truth with anyone else.

"Zelda—" he tossed the dishrag into the sink and with fast steps joined her on the sofa, taking her hand in his "—I'm so sorry to hear that, but I'm glad you're here."

She clutched his fingers tighter, soaking in his strength and the comfort of his presence. "I look back and it seems so obvious to me now what must have happened. But when I was in the middle of it, the change in him—the way he behaved—came on so gradually. Do you know the fable about the frog in a pot of water where the temperature was increased so slowly the frog didn't realize the danger until it was boiling to death? That was me."

He stayed silent, simply smoothing a thumb across her wrist, listening.

Closing her eyes for a moment almost as if she could picture the very first temperature increase, she pushed on. Perhaps speaking about it, no matter how painful, would help her regain her power. She'd given the secrets of her past far too much sway over her when she had no reason to feel shame about the relationship.

"It started with the move away from my family. Then when we arrived in Atlanta, he started his job before I began mine, so he had me deal with starting the utilities and signing the lease. Months went by before the first time he came up short on his part, and I covered the difference. Then it happened again, and again until my account was drained. He always had a good excuse that made sense in the moment."

She shook her head, another breath stinging her nostrils with the lemon-scented cleaner. "Hindsight, I can see how those shortfalls tended to come anytime we had an argument or I asserted my independence in some way. There's more, but I hate to dwell on it. You get the idea."

He nodded solemnly. "I understand."

Something in his tone said that he did. Deeply. And that gave her the encouragement, the feeling of safety, to continue. "The only time I really stood up for myself came over volunteering to groom dogs for the animal shelter."

That had been her line in the sand. She'd allowed him to dictate plenty of things in her life before that. But keeping her from the animals that needed her? That had been a last straw, helping her to recognize how unreasonable he was. How overly accommodating she'd been to someone who didn't deserve her.

"And that's where you met Maisey." His broad palm

shifted to the small pup snoozing in her bed, his hand rising and falling in even measure with each of her breaths.

"We needed each other." She adjusted a bow on top of Maisey's head, the green polka-dot ribbon perched in a twisted tuft of fur. "Both of us were isolated and hurting. I give her credit for healing me so I had the resolve to leave. I've fought hard to rebuild my life."

"I hope you know that I'm not a threat to that." His earnest gaze held hers.

"I do," she whispered, looking into his deep brown eyes.

He nodded, his thumb still caressing above her racing pulse. "Just making sure you understand that even though you tempt me so very much, this can't be more than the fake dating we signed on for."

She nibbled her bottom lip, swaying toward him, wanting his mouth on hers more than ever. "That temptation thing works both ways."

He dipped his head toward her, waiting, and she saw in his hesitation the invitation for her to make the next move. For her to choose. That made her answer feel all the more obvious. Inevitable. But oh man, did she appreciate the way he let her make that decision after how many times she'd been maneuvered in her last relationship.

So she felt the rightness of this choice. The affirmation of her own strength.

She swayed into him, giving a kiss and taking his in return. Her heart picked up speed and she slid her arms around his neck. He palmed her back, low on her spine, the warmth of his strong but gentle fingers searing through her shirt.

Ever so gently he shifted Maisey's dog bed to the side, settling her against a pile of throw pillows. How much further would this go? She only knew she wanted to follow the sensation to its conclusion.

Easing her head back, she stared into his eyes and saw an answering desire in his own. She searched for the right words to—

The cell phone buzzed on the coffee table, vibrating against the pine plank with an incoming text. Her phone. She blinked her eyes, if not her thoughts, clear and grabbed the device. Her stomach sank at the words, the message from Isobel like a bucket of ice water over her soul.

Emergency with Lottie. Doc Barnett is checking her over at the lodge clinic. May need to go to the emergency room.

Troy checked his watch, finding a half hour had passed since the call about Lottie. The thirty minutes had felt like an eternity while he waited in the lodge dining hall for word from the clinic where Doc Barnett was examining his young patient under the watchful eyes of the three sisters.

The dining hall was almost empty for once, with no pack-tivities. Only the staff walked through, clearing away the remains of dinner and dishes, the clink echoing. Worry for the little one tugged at him, *almost* crowding out thoughts of how close he and Zelda had come to tossing caution to the wind earlier. Later, he would sift through what happened and decide how to proceed.

If Zelda was even willing to proceed.

She'd dealt with a whole lot more in her previous relationship than he ever would have guessed. No doubt it would take her some time to sort through the fallout of being with someone more interested in controlling her than caring for her. He battled a surge of anger at the thought. But now wasn't the time to think about that.

Cupping a glass of tea between his hands, he looked from Cash to Gil across the table from him and asked, "What exactly happened with Lottie?"

Gil leaned forward, elbows on the table. "We were all eating dinner, nothing out of the ordinary, and the next thing we knew, Lottie got really weak and said her back hurt."

Cash scratched along his jaw, forehead furrowed with deep worry trenches. "She never complains, never. I'm just so glad Doc was here eating with his family."

Troy couldn't imagine how worried he would be if Harper was on the other side of that door, her life in danger. His gaze skimmed to where Harper sat huddled with Wynn at another table, both of them making a serious dent in a banana split. "Has Doc said anything at all?"

"We haven't heard a word from him yet," Cash answered, frustration and worry creasing his face. "It's all I can do not to just haul Lottie down the mountain to the emergency room."

Troy turned his glass round and round on the table-top. "Action is always easier than waiting for answers. I believe I'm not alone in saying that, Cash."

"I do know she's in good hands." Cash's throat moved with a deep swallow of emotion.

Gil leaned back in his wooden chair. "Thank goodness for Harper."

Troy frowned, looking to his daughter, then back again. "Harper?"

Gil nodded, his chair's front legs returning to the floor with a thud. "She's the one who noticed Lottie was growing lethargic." He waved toward the two teens at the next table. "Harper, are your ears burning? Because we're talking about you."

She looked up fast, then pushed back her chair and shuffled over, fingers tucked in her jeans' pockets. "Yeah? Is it time to go?" She gripped the back of a chair. "I was hoping we could stick around until we get an update from the doctor…"

Troy rested a palm over her grip. "We're staying. I hear you saved the day for Lottie."

She scuffed the toe of her high-tops along the wood floor. "It was nothing. I was sitting right by her."

"Well, I'm proud of you, kiddo," Troy said, noticing in that moment how grown up she'd become.

Harper blushed deep scarlet. "As long as Lottie's okay, that's what matters most. Oh, and Maisey, too. How's she feeling?"

"Much better," he said, thankful, but also feeling the need to check in on the dog again anyway. "The swelling's gone down, and she's taking a much-needed nap after all the excitement."

"That's good," Harper said, sighing with relief. "Well, I'll be sure to keep an extra-close eye on her at work tomorrow."

He wanted to tell her how proud he was to hear her take on more responsibility, but worried she might get prickly. He needed to keep the conversation on an even keel. His thoughts were cut short by the opening of the clinic door across the lobby. Doc Barnett stepped out, his shorts and T-shirt telegraphing how he'd been pulled from his casual family dinner.

Troy scraped back his chair, only a step behind Cash as they made fast strides across the entryway, meeting the doctor just outside the open clinic door. Looking over Barnett's shoulder, Troy took in the welcome sight of the three women kneeling around Lottie in her wheelchair. Their backs were turned, so he couldn't get a read on their reactions. Not that they would risk upsetting Lottie by a big display.

Troy shifted his attention back to the physician, his heart in his stomach as he waited for the verdict.

"Everything checks out alright," Doc Barnett informed Cash calmly, although a hint of concern flickered in his kind eyes. "I think it's nothing more than an upset stomach, possibly a previously undetected food allergy. She should be fine to go home this evening, but I told Isobel that I would like to see Lottie in my office downtown first thing tomorrow."

Cash's forehead furrowed. "Could a new allergy be an indication of her kidneys failing?"

Doc cupped the man's shoulder. "Let's take this one step at a time. One day at a time. And for today—or rather for tonight—we are not in a crisis."

Relief rocked Troy all the way to his boots. While it wasn't a complete clean bill of health, at least the immediate crisis seemed to have passed. Now there was nothing left but to head back to the cabin.

His gaze tracked to Zelda again as she hitched her backpack over her shoulders. She'd had a day full of worries, no question. Would she be riding home with her sister—or would she be going with him in the truck?

More importantly, where did things stand between them after he took his daughter home? He couldn't deny he wanted to pick up where he and Zelda had left off before the phone rang. To launch back into that kiss and take it to the explosive conclusion they'd been battling since they met.

Chapter Thirteen

Relieved and exhausted, Zelda stood with Troy outside the ranch's main lodge. This day had been a roller coaster of emotions, and she couldn't help but want to curl up against his broad chest to sleep.

And more.

The dark mountain night still managed to surprise her after so long living in the city. Moonbeams barely pierced through the thick umbrella of trees. Porch lights and the flickering of electric tiki torches offered faint relief, along with the occasional glow of car lights. Few drove around the ranch, other than staff, most guests walking from their cabin to dinner or events. It made for peaceful evenings.

Troy fished in his jeans pocket for his key fob. "I'll bring the truck around. I know your ankle's getting better, but you've had a long day on your feet."

"Thank you," she said, her face warm with emotions of all kinds as she stared at him. Longing and regret fought for dominance. "I hope you understand that we can't, uh, finish the date. I need to be with my sister and help her settle Lottie for the night."

"Of course, I understand," he said, reaching back to gently squeeze her shoulder. "Family is everything."

"I agree." She just wished she hadn't let so much time lapse in connecting with her sisters before coming to Moonlight Ridge. She hated that she'd allowed herself to be isolated from the people who meant the most to her. Knowing that Troy understood and shared her values meant more to her than she would have imagined. "About earlier... This fake dating is more difficult to navigate than I expected."

A wry grin kicked a dimple into one cheek. "That's an understatement."

"The community here is so tight knit, anything we do ripples." She glanced over her shoulder, then back. "It'll be a balancing act not to let the gossip get out of hand."

An obvious, but important point, especially since Zelda would be staying here, continuing to build a new life for herself after he left.

He raised a hand. "No need to say anything more. We can talk about it later, when emotions aren't running so high."

Was that regret she saw chasing across his face? It was difficult to tell in the dim light, but she recognized the feeling inside herself. It was more than just attraction. He intrigued her, enticed her in a way she hadn't felt before...

The front door to the lodge flung open and Harper plowed through, Wynn close behind.

"Dad? Dad," Harper called out before coming to a breathless halt beside him. "Could I go get Maisey and take her to our cabin?" She turned to Zelda, a tentative smile softening her face. "Maisey could spend the night, if my dad doesn't mind. Then you won't have to worry about her while you're helping with Lottie."

He looked to Zelda, leaving it to her to decide.

Zelda hooked an arm with Harper. "That would be a great help. Thank you."

"It's no big deal. We all live close to each other." She shuffled her feet. "I know things are okay for Lottie tonight, but what about later? If she can't get the donor she needs?"

The fears in Harper's eyes echoed all the same ones chasing around inside her.

Zelda drew in a shaky breath. "Let's just take things one day at a time. Like Doc Barnett said."

Wise words that she needed to heed on many levels, including where Troy was concerned. Today, something had shifted between them, at least on her part when she'd opened up about her past. Troy's sensitivity and understanding revealed surprising layers under his tough cowboy veneer.

And somehow that made him all the more irresistible at a time when she was feeling far too emotional.

Hiking along the darkened path later that night, Troy stuffed his hands in his pockets, needing to burn off the adrenaline. At least Lottie was alright—for now. Even though the upset stomach seemed rooted in a newly discovered food allergy, the evening's scare served as a reminder of the child's precarious health. He was grateful that Zelda had called with an update that the little girl was resting comfortably after she helped Isobel get her settled in for the night.

But the child's health scare had made him realize how much the Daltons had come to mean to him in a short time. He didn't have much of a past to reference when it came to family, but he knew enough to recognize these sisters shared a special bond with each other and those they loved.

Overhead, a crescent moon offered soft light as he picked his way down the path. Hoots trilled in the distance as he passed a stately oak tree whose trunk was adorned with a paw-shaped sign: It's a Wonderfur World.

Boots crunching in the loose gravel of the trail, he sucked in a deep breath of mountain air. Harper had walked Maisey, then fluffed her dog bed twice before tucking her in with an extra treat. He was reminded yet again that he needed to get her a pet of her own. Of course, that would be easier once they'd settled into their new place. It didn't make sense to get a puppy now when they had a move in their future. Ironic that he'd gone from craving the travel of the rodeo circuit to yearning to put down roots.

All thoughts for tomorrow.

Right now, he was free to take his time doing— nothing. Just put one foot in front of the other. The idleness was a rarity. He let the quiet settle the unease inside him, passing by a dark cabin, the moonlight glinting off the window drawn with shades. Another paw-print plaque read Anything's Paw-sible.

A deer rustled in the brush to his left. Troy stopped

as a doe bolted, leaping across the trail. The white tail disappeared from sight as the doe maneuvered through the sycamores and oaks.

A voice whispered through the night, then louder. "Troy?"

Zelda. He paused in his tracks, pivoting on the dirt trail, his boots cushioned by fallen pine needles. And, of course, he shouldn't be surprised that he'd somehow wound his way toward her cabin.

He found her sitting on her porch rocker, the light casting her in a warm glow. "You're still awake. I would have thought you would have crashed by now."

"I could say the same about you."

With slow strides, he closed the distance between them and opened her gate. A few short weeks ago, he would have wondered if he would be welcome. Things had shifted between them.

Climbing the steps, he took in the sight of her in frayed jean shorts and a sweatshirt to combat the cool mountain night. Her legs stretched in front of her, slim and toned, her feet in fuzzy striped socks. The air between them crackled with the unspoken memories of their kiss, but he didn't want to assume anything or pressure her.

He cleared his throat as he stopped in front of her. "I was just out taking a long walk. I needed to air out my thoughts when the world is quiet."

"Have a seat if you have time." She motioned for him to have the other rocking chair. "Where's Harper?"

"Asleep." He lowered himself onto the rustic pine

rocker. "I set the alarm when I left. If anyone tries to go in or out, my phone will give me an alert."

Zelda wriggled her toes in her colorful socks. "How did our parents ever keep track of us without modern technology?"

"I'm starting to think that wasn't a bad thing," he said wryly.

She chuckled softly. "So, why are you really out and about 'airing out your thoughts'? Is there something weighing on your mind that you would like to share?"

"I was just walking off excess adrenaline after the scare with Lottie. Thank heaven it wasn't anything worse."

"I understand the feeling," she said, her voice husky with emotion as she toyed with the hem of her purple sweatshirt. "I wouldn't have minded a walk myself."

Was she only referring to Lottie…or was she hinting at more?

He glanced at her foot and didn't see any swelling—as best he could check through the fuzzy cotton. "How's your ankle holding up after the long day?"

"It's doing well, but I don't want to push my luck." She tipped her head back against the rocker, her breasts pressing enticingly against the purple sweatshirt with a grooming school logo. "I should probably start out with something like some horseback riding."

Horseback riding? His attention shifted from her chest to a possible opening to see her again soon. "You're talking to the right person. I can hook you up anytime. Just let me know."

"What about tomorrow morning?" she asked

promptly, with a playful light in her eyes. The playful light almost covered a serious glint, a weightiness that this request went beyond fake dating. "I've got a light load at the salon and don't need to sign in until lunchtime."

Her timing couldn't have been better since Harper had plans to meet up with a group of teens at the lodge—Wynn and some others she'd met zip-lining.

Standing, he took her hand and knelt at her feet. "Your wish is my command, m'lady."

Her fingers clenched around his, her skin soft against his. More of that awareness snapped between them like an unbroken current, one that drew him closer. The sting increased, the ache of wanting her growing as he drew nearer.

He tucked his knuckle under her chin, tipping her face up toward his. Then he waited, staring into her deep blue eyes, the pupils widening with desire. Her lips parted and she swayed toward him, her breath puffing over him with warmth and a hint of peppermint.

Moving closer to kiss was as natural as breathing. He couldn't remember when he'd felt so connected to another woman, especially one he'd known for such a short time, but there was no denying the power of their attraction to one another.

But he didn't want to assume where things would lead next. Once again, he needed to leave this up to her. And no sooner than he'd entertained the thought than she stood without ending the embrace, drawing him to his feet along with her.

Instead, she deepened the contact, her hand gripping his shoulders as she pressed closer. "Take me inside."

He eased back and stared in her eyes, searching. "Are you sure this is what you want?"

"Tonight?" she answered breathlessly. "Yes, I am absolutely certain."

She clasped him by both hands, backing up as she tugged him through the living room toward her bedroom, her eyes glinting with passion and determination.

Step for step, he followed her down the hall, their treads softened by the braid runner. "And tomorrow?"

"Do we have to think about that?" She paused outside her bedroom door.

He cradled her face in his hands. "As long as you're sure you won't have regrets."

She covered his hands with hers. "We've both wanted this since the moment we met. I'm one hundred percent certain that this window of time is meant for the two of us."

He'd thought as much, but hearing her voice the desire ramped the passion inside him. "You've wanted me since the moment we met?"

Her smile crinkled her nose and lit her blue eyes like a flame as she clasped the doorknob and twisted. "Are you angling for a compliment?"

Following her through the door into her vanilla-scented room with a welcoming bed, he vowed, "I'm angling for *you*."

The next morning, Zelda clasped the reins of her sorrel quarter horse, a gelding named Dakota. The horse's sure-footed hooves clopped against the grass and rocks as they descended along the narrow mountain path back toward the valley. Her gaze stayed glued on Troy ahead of her, riding Lyra, the white tail swishing. The broad expanse of his back called to her, making her yearn for a return to what they'd shared the night before.

Tipping her face upward, she soaked in the rising sun. She drew in deep breaths of honeysuckle-scented breeze, savored the sound of a blue jay calling to its mate. Her senses were on high alert after making love with Troy last night. Living in the moment, she refused to let anything spoil her mood.

This time with Troy felt like a date—a real date—and she didn't want to think about how, in less than two weeks, the junior rodeo would be past, his employment here at an end. If she landed the job opening at the ranch, she would be staying. Plans would be made for their separate futures. Shifting her weight in her saddle, she did her best to ignore her increasing anxiety about the clock ticking away.

The path widened and Troy slowed his mount from a leisurely trot to an ambling walk until they rode alongside each other. "You're quite at ease in the saddle. I'm impressed."

"I'll take that as high praise, coming from you. I'm a far cry from rodeo material, though." Her hands tightened around the braided reins as Dakota stepped over a mostly decomposed tree trunk, moss and fungi covering the bark.

Nearly walking in stride, each horse regained their

smooth pace as the broad trailed opened to soft green grass. The clop, clop of the hoofbeats soothed like a metronome in time with the musical trickle of water down a sheer rock face.

His smile crinkled the corners of his eyes. "You're as pretty as any rodeo queen I've ever seen."

"Well, aren't you a smooth talker?" she teased, enjoying the easy flirtation.

"Only with you," he answered with a seriousness that went beyond simple banter. Resting his hand on the saddle horn, he leaned back in his seat as the trail's decline steepened. She mirrored the way he moved his body, guiding Dakota as birds cackled above their heads. "I know that we both have important reasons not to get involved in a relationship right now. But I was wondering if you would object if I stayed in touch after I move. I'll only be a few hours away. Not an insurmountable drive."

A nervous twinge skittered through her, like little pebbles rolling down a drop-off on the path into a dangerous plunge. She wasn't sure if her nerves came from the thought of a relationship, his move or the possibility of a long-distance commitment that would pull her away from her family.

Maybe her nerves stemmed from all three.

She wanted their light flirting back. Couldn't they indulge in a simple day without worries or decisions?

"I'll think about it," she said evasively, searching for anything else to discuss.

Dakota's ears pricked. Alert. Noticing her shift in mood no doubt.

Zelda cast a glance skyward, sun washing over her face. "For now, I need to focus on searching for a donor for Lottie. I also promised my sister I would do a deep dive into some old county records that were salvaged and later scanned. We're hoping it might give a lead to finding the baby Gran gave up for adoption."

Would Troy notice she was babbling to avoid what *he* wanted to talk about?

He studied her for a few heartbeats. His eyes sharp beneath the shadow of his Stetson, he guided his palomino around a boulder. Their paths diverged slightly as the trail opened wider still. Dakota's steps quickened, a trot breaking out.

She pulled twice on the reins to settle him back down. "It would be an answer to all our prayers if Gran's lost child could be the donor." She breathed a sigh of relief that he didn't seem inclined to pressure her. "I heard from my sister that they had a couple of walk-ins come by Doc Barnett's office to get tested as possible donors. Apparently last night's scare with Lottie generated talk—and action."

"I'm relieved to hear it." Troy reached down to pat the neck of his mare as she stayed steady and even-keeled when a rogue squirrel whizzed by. Dakota side-stepped, shying from the furry creature. "You and your sisters are a force of nature. I'm confident you'll leave no stone unturned."

"My sisters maybe." She shrugged aside the compliment. Praise had always left her feeling uneasy. "They've always been go-getters. Look at how Isobel has turned her gift for writing into such a powerful blog, spreading awareness for persons with disabilities. And, of course, Neve is a genius."

"And you've got a gift with handling animals," he reminded her.

"I wasn't fishing for a compliment." The unsettled sensation that had started during his talk of long-distance relationships multiplied, and once again she found herself searching for a way to divert the discussion. She took in the sign on the tree, shaped like a running dog, captioned: Chase Your Dream.

Perfect. "Tell me about your plans for the training center. I want to hear about your dream—in the interest of our shared love of animals."

"Much like we've done here this summer leading up to the junior rodeo, I want to train young riders in the sport."

"Like a summer camp?" she prompted, thankful that he was talking so she could regain her equilibrium.

"More than that. More of a year-round program for the under-eighteen crowd. The facility will also host events and..." He paused. "I'm rambling."

"Not at all. I'm enjoying every word." Even though she'd asked as a distraction, she truly was interested in hearing more. If only that didn't serve as a reminder of his leaving. "It's clearly your passion."

"If we're talking about passions," he said with a devilish gleam in his eyes. Both of them still in the saddle, he leaned to press a lingering kiss, stroking the nape of her neck lightly before straightening again. "As much as I wish we could linger here..."

Gulping, she nodded, her world totally topsy-turvy

again. "I need to get back to work and so do you." She leaned to graze her lips over his once more, all the while wishing he didn't tempt her so. Then she straightened, digging her heels into her horse's sides. "Catch me if you can."

Dakota perked, powerful hindquarters digging into the ground. Upturned muddy earth flew behind her, the scent of fresh dirt momentarily noticeable until he launched into a headlong gallop. A laugh tore from her chest as she guided the horse onward.

Troy's own answering laugh washed over her, Lyra a lightning flash approaching like a summer storm. In a few strides, he'd caught up with her. Lyra started pulling forward.

Deepening her seat, she clicked to Dakota, catapulting him ahead. They thundered through the open stretch of land that led back toward the ranch. As sure as she heard hoofbeats, she knew that time was chasing them and would soon win, leaving them both the losers as saying goodbye would be all the tougher.

But for now, she couldn't stop herself from making the most of every day they had left together.

Chapter Fourteen

Wynn just wanted the day to end so he could start fresh. But for now he had to trudge through the rest of his work shift and pretend he didn't feel totally stupid for mixing up the feed for the horses. He'd been so sure that every single horse needed a mixture of alfalfa cubes, spirulina and regular feed. It turned out only Patch, an Appaloosa mare, needed the mixture. At least Troy had caught him before he actually dumped it all into each of the feed bins.

Still, it was embarrassing.

Shoving the memory down, Wynn started to check the spacing on the distance between barrels for tomorrow's junior rodeo. Dirt kicked up around him as he looked at the number on the tape measure. Rocking the red-and-white-striped barrel, he moved it slightly back.

Hopefully, he wouldn't screw up again. And if he did? Troy wouldn't be around to see it this time, since he'd just left to get more barrels and portable fencing.

There were lots of other folks still helping out, but he only cared about Harper.

His gaze skated across the small arena toward her. Yellow rag in hand as she polished a black leather show saddle, she looked hot—as always—in her jeans and high-tops, her concert T-shirt inching up to show a stripe of her stomach. Except the longer he looked at her, the more he realized that her shoulders were slumped. He couldn't see her expression since she wore a ball cap and it made shadows over her face.

Winding the tape measure back up before tucking it into his left front pocket, he strode across the dirt floor. Hands in his back pockets, he stopped just short of her. "I thought you had a shift at the grooming salon today."

"Nah," she said, keeping her face hidden as she worked at some scuffs on the fancy saddle flap. The light scent of saddle soap and high-quality leather wafted in the air. "Zelda's foot is doing better so she sent me over here to help out some."

He dipped his head to see...her eyes were sheened with tears, her mouth downturned.

"Hey, what's wrong?" he asked, resting a hand on her shoulder.

She scrubbed her wrist over her eyes before looking up. "Something's up with my dad over the past week. Like since Lottie had that scary stomach thing." She sat on a hay bale, shoulders slouching even more. "Thank goodness it was nothing, but my dad's still acting weird."

"What do you mean something's up with your father?" He sat beside her, his knee pressed against hers. "I thought you two were getting along better."

"He's been...busy lately," she said, her voice soft and sad as she placed the cloth on the deep seat of the saddle. "Like gone a lot."

"So? He has a job." Which was better than his old man 50 percent of the time, when he wasn't getting fired for being late because he was too hungover. "Your dad works like almost all the time."

"Yeah, he's schmoozing with the Levi guy to start a business my mom will absolutely hate." She chewed her bottom lip before continuing, "Not that my dad is thinking about my mom. He and Zelda went whitewater rafting and to campfire karaoke. They even drove downtown to pick up supplies and they stayed for supper out. He gets to have a life, but I don't. It's not fair."

He frowned, struggling to follow her train of thought. "I thought you said your mom and dad are divorced. Only makes sense he will have a girlfriend sometime."

"He says it's not serious, but I know better."

The longer she talked, the tougher it was to sympathize. Stuff came so easy for Harper. She made great grades in school. Her dad helped her with homework and kept the pantry full. And she didn't have to go back to a miserable school life at the end of the summer.

Unable to hold in all the hurt and the frustration, he blurted, "Do you have any idea how lucky you are?"

She straightened, her eyes blinking fast. "Excuse me? I'm not sure what you mean."

Put on the spot, he wished he could call back the words, but it was too late to call them back. Besides, he'd meant it. Maybe she really didn't understand how fortunate she'd gotten to have Troy for a dad. "I get that your mom left and that really sucks. Everybody knows she's not coming back and I think you know it, too, but that doesn't mean she's gone out of your life. You complain and trash-talk your dad, and for the life of me, I can't seem to figure out what he's done that's so awful."

She grabbed his arm and squeezed, fingertips wrapping around his blue plaid sleeve. "He's like my jailer. No wonder Mom left."

Wynn stared at her angry face and even knowing she was just hurt didn't make it much better. Right now, he was kinda wondering what he'd even seen in her. Hurt or not, she had a princess, spoiled life.

"He cares where you are. He worries about you. I would give anything to have a parent that gave a crap about me when I'm hurting." Swallowing a big lump in his throat, he looked back to the bags of alfalfa and spirulina, and thought about how Mr. Troy didn't call him stupid. Not for an honest mistake. Instead, he'd explained what each supplement did and why only certain horses needed them. "Or to have one who would help me with my school, rather than just getting mad at my bad grades."

She shot to her feet, shoes stomping. "Well, if I'm so horrible, then why are you hanging out with me?"

His heart tugged for her a little. But not enough to back down. "I don't believe you're a bad person. I just think you don't notice how awful things are for other people." Wynn scuffed his boot against the ground. "Like sometimes you forget to count your blessings."

She sat beside him again, some of the mad seeming to seep out of her. "Are things bad for you at home?

I'm sorry that I didn't think to ask you more about yourself."

The last thing he wanted to talk about was his sad-sack life. "We're not talking about me."

Harper tugged at the sleeve of his flannel shirt gently, toying with the rolled-up cuff. "Well, I want to know anyway."

"It's not a home—a family—like yours where you get supported." He looked around the arena, filled with the scent of hay and horses, hard work and people who cared. "That's why being here is so important to me. I'm happy and building my future with this internship. There'll be scouts at the rodeo tomorrow and if I'm lucky, it'll open up some doors for me. As much as I like you, I can't afford to derail this opportunity."

"You're breaking up with me," she whispered, her voice shocked and shaking.

And even though he hadn't planned that when he started talking to her today, now he recognized the truth in her words. There was no future for him with her, not even in a friendship. He needed to focus and move on.

He picked up her hand and held it one last time. "I'm letting you go and you're doing the same for me."

The day before the rodeo, Troy hauled bale after bale of hay off the back of his truck for the competition and after-party decor. The familiar sounds of quick orders and horse snuffles echoed around him. Anticipation had a scent all its own, a sweet and earthy energy.

He should be excited about the event, the chance

to shine and promote his dream in front of Levi. The event promised to be a major success. But every moment away from Zelda, he found himself thinking only of when he would see her next. The past week together had been anything but simple and no strings, spending every moment together whenever his daughter was busy elsewhere.

Except the more time he spent with Zelda, the more he realized he didn't want their relationship to end once his summer gig here wrapped up. If only the financing paperwork from Levi wasn't ready and waiting. Everything he'd been hoping and planning for was coming to fruition.

And yet, his stomach was filled with dread.

These past days with Zelda had been some of the best he'd known. Her adventurous spirit had been on full display when they'd gone whitewater rafting. On their trip into town, her work ethic had been undeniable. And how could he not be enchanted by her playful spirit during campfire karaoke? He didn't want to end their time together.

He hefted up another bale of hay and started to fling it out of the pickup bed—only to pause as his daughter shot out of the arena's double doors. "Hey, now. Careful, girl."

Chin jutting, she stopped short, face impassive at first glance. In the morning sun, he saw a tremor on her lips. The smallest indication of pain. "Oh, I didn't see you there."

He dropped the bale and vaulted from the back of the truck to the ground. "What's wrong?"

She put her fists on her hips, looking like the toddler version of herself who'd been denied a second helping of her favorite ice cream. "What do you think?"

"I honestly haven't a clue." He'd been giving her more freedom lately. Wasn't that what she'd wanted?

"Nobody tells me anything," she cried, voice wobbling in a gust of summer wind. Her eyes—his eyes—lined with the promise of tears.

He wanted to hug her but sensed that she would just pull away. So he swallowed down his frustration and asked, "What do you mean?"

"I'm not fooled by all the time you're spending with Zelda," she said, spitting out the words. Her chest heaved. "And I saw you with that Levi guy this week, the big shot with all the money. You're still planning to move again, aren't you?"

He felt like he was trapped in a pinball machine trying to keep up with the rapid shifts in her conversation. Best to pick them off, one at a time. He opted to start with the Levi subject, since he didn't even have a cohesive answer for himself when it came to his feelings for Zelda. "Kiddo, I have to pay the bills. The new facility is an investment in our future."

Crossing her arms over her chest, she slumped against the truck. "You brought me to the middle of nowhere, away from my friends. No wonder Mom doesn't want anything to do with us. She hates this way of life."

This didn't seem the time to point out that her mother had been distancing herself from them for years. Specifically since he'd taken a job at a horse-breeding farm to give them stability in hopes of saving the family unit. With a decent-size house, a yard for making memories, fairly predictable hours. All of the things his wife had argued that she'd wanted. The whole nine yards. He'd cut back drastically on his rodeo time.

It hadn't worked. His own frustration rumbled in his chest as he shifted in his boots, taking a step closer, keeping his voice gentle and low. "I think you know that the marriage ending would have happened no matter where we lived."

She hitched her foot back and kicked the tire behind her again and again. "I guess crummy relationship luck is in my genes."

Ah, now he thought he understood the cause of her bad mood. Adjusting his Stetson, he asked, "Did something happen with Wynn?"

Her chest heaved faster and faster, her eyes watering. "He just pretended to be interested because I'm your daughter and he thinks you're *amazing*."

Seeing those two tears roll down her cheek brought all his protective papa bear instincts to the fore. Troy stifled the urge to go demand the boy apologize for whatever he'd done to hurt Harper, but he had a feeling he was only getting half the story.

Maybe his parental instincts were sharpening after all. "Did he tell you he was trying to gain favor with me? Because if so, chasing my daughter is the exact opposite way to get any positive attention from me."

"Ha. Ha," she said sarcastically, swiping her eyes. "So funny. Not."

His shoulders braced. "Harper, I'm trying to be patient and sympathetic, but I draw the line at blatant disrespect."

"Respect?" she cried, pushing away from the truck. "You want my respect after what you've done?"

Breathing in the musk of hay and dirt, he did his best to keep his voice calm but firm. "I've already explained we had to come here this summer because of my job. Keeping a roof over our head is mighty important."

"I'm not talking about that," she wailed, jabbing her finger at him. "*You* made Mom leave. You're the reason we're not a family anymore. She hates this way of life just as much as I do."

And before he could pull the stunned look off his face, she stormed off, running away from the arena and toward their cabin. He'd known she was struggling, but he'd thought they were making progress, that the Moonlight Ridge magic was easing the strain between them. But he'd vastly underestimated the depth of her pain. He knew she needed time to cool down or he might have thought about going after her. Perhaps they both needed a little space.

Not to mention, he had a major event to prepare for. He scrubbed the hand over his face.

He'd tried his best and seemed to have failed at every turn. Although how could he blame Harper after all the upheaval? He hadn't been much of a role model either when it came to stable relationships. Going from a divorce to no-strings dating while traveling.

And in his first real dating relationship with Zelda, he hadn't been up-front with his daughter. Or Zelda.

Or even himself.

He wasn't sure yet how to handle the outburst with his daughter, but he did know he didn't want to say goodbye to Zelda when he left Moonlight Ridge.

Zelda had never thought of herself as a greedy person. Certainly her sisters had always insisted she was generous to a fault.

But as time counted down for Troy to leave the dude ranch, she found herself stealing every moment possible to be with him. She put her vintage VW Bug in Park outside the arena, the back seat full of grooming supplies to gussy up the horses for tomorrow's show. She'd brought flowers and ribbons, combs and clips. And yes, she could have waited until tomorrow, but she expected the day would be hectic and she wanted to see Troy.

She hip-bumped her front door closed, scanning the grounds for a sign of him. As she strode toward the door to the show arena, she sidestepped fast as Harper raced past without so much as a sideways glance. Strange. And not like the teen at all.

Turning back toward the arena's metal building, Zelda slammed into a masculine chest. A familiar masculine chest.

Troy.

She flattened her palms to the warm, muscular wall. "What was that all about with Harper?"

Folding his hands over hers, he squeezed once before lowering them away. "She's upset."

"I would say so." She laced their fingers together,

even though she felt self-conscious for having touched him in the middle of their workspace. Indeed, the dude ranch was a flurry of activity. Coworkers were setting up decorations for pop-up concession stands, stocking areas beyond the wooden ordering countertops with cans of sodas and sparkling water. "Did she tell you why?"

"She had a list," he said, his cheeks puffing with an exasperated sigh, "much of which was focused on the move, then the new training center and how my way of life made her mother leave."

Guilt pinched as she thought of their earlier vow not to get involved, for Harper's sake. How quickly they'd tossed those good intentions aside to the enchanting summer wind.

Zelda fiddled with her paw charm as two workers carried a giant red cowboy hat made of wood and placed it atop a neat stack of hay. "Is she upset over us seeing each other?"

"She mentioned it, but only briefly. She was more focused on her mother. And on me." Worry stamped his features as he stared in the direction his daughter had taken. "The girl's a roller coaster of emotions. One minute she seems settled in the routine she and I have established, and the next she's back to idealizing her mother."

More guilt piled on top of the belly full she already felt. And to further complicate matters, she resented the woman for never once calling Harper in all the time Zelda had known her. The wreckage left in that teen's life had been substantial.

"Poor Harper," she said, lowering her voice as more employees passed with supplies in hand, heading toward the stage with a big banner proclaiming Raise the Woof. "I hate this for her."

"Me, too," he said through gritted teeth. "Then to make things worse, she and Wynn broke up."

Her hand flew to her chest as she gasped. "What horrible timing. I'll let you go so you can chase after her."

He shook his head, eyes still focused on the trail where Harper had disappeared. "One thing I do know about my kid, she needs some time to cool down before we talk."

"Okay," Zelda said haltingly. She would have to trust him as the parent, but she still didn't like to think of Harper alone and so distraught.

Troy slid an arm around her shoulders, surprising her out of her thoughts. "Zelda, thank you for listening, and for caring. I may not have all the answers when it comes to Harper, but her outburst helped me focus on one very important thing."

She leaned into the warmth of him. So much for keeping their distance. "What would that be?"

"Harper needs more stability and predictability in her life."

"Agreed," Zelda said cautiously, fidgeting with the hem of her T-shirt. Was he breaking things off? They'd only planned to be together until he left at the end of the summer, but feeling the end approach made her stomach clench all the same.

"So, what I mentioned during our ride last week

about trying a long-distance romance," he said in the most logical of voices. "I really think we should give it a chance. Things are going so well between us and it will be one less goodbye in Harper's life."

The nerves inside her shifted from sadness to disillusionment as he narrowed their relationship to something so...practical. The emotions jumbled together until she could barely form words, but then he was saying plenty for both of them, continuing with his plan.

"I won't be moving all that far away." He cupped her shoulder, drawing her closer to his side as he made his pitch. "Only a few hours. And, if you're open to it, when your job here finishes this summer, there's a Top Dog branch outside of Nashville. Maybe they might have an opening for you..."

A roaring in her ears grew as people darted around the grounds, setting up the pop-up shop tents. Her mouth was dry. She pressed her fingers to his lips, unable to listen any longer as her dreams lay shattered at her feet.

"Troy, I realize that you mean this in the best of ways." She had to give him at least that much benefit of the doubt. He wasn't a bad man. He just couldn't be her forever man. Not if he understood so little about her and her hard-won independence. "I can't uproot my life again for someone to chase their dreams. I'm chasing mine now."

She hadn't realized how fully committed she was to the idea until this moment. And it felt right, even though it meant there would be no chance for her to be with Troy. She had to forge her own path now. "I'm home. Here with my family. I've already applied for the full-time groomer opening this fall, and Hollie has told me I'm their top pick."

He stared down at her in shock, easing her hand away from his mouth. "So that's it, then."

Her heart squeezed in her chest, and she so deeply wanted to throw caution to the wind, to do anything to keep this man. But she knew that wasn't the path to happiness. Not for either of them. "I'm sad to be saying goodbye to you—and to Harper as well. Sadder than I can put into words. But yes, that's how it has to be."

Chapter Fifteen

Troy watched Zelda walk away from him, her limp barely perceptible, and felt his heart split in two. Only a short time earlier today, he'd been making plans for a long-distance romance.

An invitation she'd thrown back in his face.

In short order, he'd wrecked his relationship with his daughter, and any hopes of a future with Zelda. He bit back a curse of frustration.

Taking one deep breath, then a second, he forced himself to focus on the tasks to accomplish instead of the wreckage of his personal life. The clatter of voices by his truck caught his attention. Two of the stable hands, young men in their early twenties, started unloading the unwieldy bales of hay.

Troy debated stepping in to help, but the workers quickly fell into a rhythm, better adjusting to the weight of the bales as they continued. A strange heaviness rocked his chest as he left the stable hands to their work, heading for the indoor arena where other ranch staff were busy setting everything up to his specifications. For the past couple of months, he had looked forward to preparing for the junior rodeo. Not so much now.

The ranch's arena had been a pleasant surprise when he'd accepted this summer gig. Sure, the ranch had an impressive spread of barns and stables, but this space offered a superb option for the junior rodeo. After which, there would be a costume party for the adults, hosted in a barn. He'd had such high hopes for celebrating with Zelda, then penciling in dates on the calendar for their future. His chest ached at the hollow her goodbye had left inside him.

Moving through the indoor arena to the barn beyond, he glanced at each of the horse's food, triple-checking Wynn's work. While no horse would have been harmed by the intern's mistake this time, learning to be attentive to the unique requirements of each horse was vital. Slacking could have serious consequences for the health and well-being of the animals under their care down the line.

He hated to call the kid on the carpet about his work since he looked like a kicked puppy every time he messed up. But Troy also wanted to remind the boy if he thought less about Harper and more about the job, he might not make these sloppy errors.

Truth be told, Troy could relate. An image of Zelda sitting on her porch flashed before his eyes. Her easy smile as she listened to him. The challenge in her eyes when she galloped down the trail.

As quick as the thoughts came to him, he shoved them aside. His bad mood was making him angry at the world, when he had no one but himself to blame for entering a relationship that couldn't possibly continue. He would be better served working himself into a stupor so he would be able to sleep tonight rather than toss and turn thinking of a future without Zelda.

He heard footsteps behind him and hauled his attention back to the present, pivoting away from the bins in time to see Cash and Gil approaching down the center aisle of the stables.

Cash leaned forward to peer into the bins as a dapple-gray horse lazily munched on loose hay, dark eyes soft. "Good to see Wynn has that all straightened out. There are times I could swear that boy has dyslexia or something like that."

A learning disability? Troy turned the thought over in his mind, wondering... The boy's application for the internship had definitely been granted based on his skills, not his grades. Troy scratched the back of his neck. Had he missed something about the teen out of his own distraction?

Cash moved to the next stall, where Lyra noisily gulped water. She looked up with a little head toss before whinnying clear and loud. "Sorry to break up your evening out with Zelda when Lottie was sick. Although the two of you seemed to have more than made up for it."

Forehead furrowed, Gil stood across the way stroking a young bay horse. A knowing smile broke out, wild as a horse turned loose in a pasture. "I thought you were on a dating hiatus for the summer.

"Well, uh, yes," Troy said, uncomfortable with the reminder of how far he'd strayed from his intentions. "I took this summer gig at the ranch to spend time with my daughter and to impress possible investors in my training facility. But Zelda… Things happened. Then they didn't. We're not an item."

"Sorry to hear that." Gil fished a molasses oat treat from his pocket. Palm flat, he offered the snack to the bay horse. "Because you're moving soon?"

Lyra whinnied again, sticking her head out of the stall, and Troy took a treat from Gil for Lyra. "There was a time I thought a long-distance relationship might have been an option. But that's not fair to her."

Gil nodded as Cash moved into the well-lit tack room. Gil's boots echoing on the cement followed. No doubt to make sure the saddles were all accounted for. Troy pulled out his tablet to double-check the event lineup.

Part of him wished he could simply throw himself into some manual labor in the barn, sweating, muscles straining. He would welcome the distraction from how time was ticking down to when he would leave to launch his plans. How had he gone from a simple summer job to letting himself get tangled up with Zelda? He'd been clear with her and himself from the start. She'd been equally up-front in those first days when they'd met.

Sparks had flown between them, but their resolve had been stronger…

Waving aside the help of the shop manager so she could assist others, he made his way to the display table featuring crystal jewelry made from gemstones mined out of the Sulis Springs Cave. Bypassing a tray of rings, he trailed his fingers along necklaces dan-

gling from a long dowel. A small plaque noted credit: Gems by River Jack.

A pink stone set in a flower charm caught his attention. Perfect. He reached, only to have his hand collide with another.

"Sorry," he said, looking up to find... "Oh, you."

Zelda jerked back her hand as if burned—her cheeks flaming red. "Oh, uh, you, too."

He jammed his hands in his pockets, blurting, "Are you following me?"

Not his most subtle statement, but she kept showing up and he didn't want her to get the wrong idea from that impulsive kiss. He needed to put a stop to things before they spiraled out of control.

That heat on her face fired in her eyes now. "You have got to be kidding me. I'm here buying a gift for my niece. I could ask if you are following me."

Two older gentlemen shopping by the carved cigar boxes shot disapproving stares his way. They were right, of course. He hadn't sounded very gentlemanly— and he didn't need the gossip.

Troy stepped around the display table, his shoulders blocking the rest of the store from watching in on their conversation. "Sorry," he said softly. "It just seems... suspicious that you're here."

Zelda jabbed him in the chest with one finger. "Listen up, Mr. Cowboy Ego. I am not following you." She poked again for each point. "I'm not trying to pin you down and steal your ever-lovin' freedom because of one silly kiss. It didn't mean any more to me than it did to you."

Finished, she folded her arms over her chest. Her very pretty chest, gentle curves only inches away.

Eyes up. "*Zelda, I apologize for that moment—*"

"*That kiss.*"

"*Fine,*" *he said through gritted teeth.* "*Yes, that kiss. I'm not sure what came over me.*"

"*My undeniable charms, no doubt.*" *Her smile was slow and dark with irony.*

"*This isn't funny,*" *he hissed, glancing behind him to make sure no one overheard.* "*I was here looking for a gift for my daughter since I've been so busy this week. I'm a single dad with no time for a fling.*"

"*A fling? Excuse me? I'm not interested in a fling, especially not with you. Let's both forget it ever happened.*" *She extended a hand.* "*Deal?*"

The air hung heavy between them with charged emotions, from their sparring and kiss. His chest pumped faster as he hauled in deep breaths filled with the scent of nearby candles and her.

This woman was a dangerous temptation he could ill afford. Troy clasped her hand in his, steeling himself to ignore the skin-to-skin sensation. "*Deal.*"

Pivoting away hard and fast, he hightailed it out of the gift shop and into the late-day foot traffic. Only to realize that he'd been so caught up in seeing Zelda, he'd forgotten all about buying Harper a necklace. Time to get his priorities back in order.

From this point going forward, he would do his level best to make sure he and Zelda Dalton crossed paths as little as possible...

* * *

The sound of horse snorts and rattling tackle brought him back to the present, but the memory of that day with Zelda lingered. Would she always torment his thoughts this much? Or would it be easier once he moved away?

Somehow, he didn't think so.

Setting aside his tablet, he started toward the double doors leading from the stable to the arena, Cash and Gil following. A forklift operator beeped and adjusted, hefting a box of confetti to be released at the end of the event.

Once the vehicle passed, Troy waved the two men to continue with him as they began hefting sound equipment from a pallet onto the stage.

They worked in tandem for a long moment until Cash broke the silence. "Tell us more about this facility that's pulling you away from us. You've mentioned it before but not in great detail."

Troy summoned up the words, his excitement over the project seriously lagging today. "It's a pretty straightforward training facility. I'll get to do the part of rodeo life that I enjoy most, without the hassle of being on the road. My daughter needs me to be there for her."

Cash scrubbed a hand over his jaw. "The rodeo circuit is no place to bring up a kid, that's for sure."

Troy hauled a long spool of an industrial extension cord from the pallet. He'd tried taking Harper on the road with him and homeschooling her last spring. The travel was supposed to have been an education, too.

But Harper had wanted the regular high school experiences—friends, going to a dance, stuff like that.

He wanted that for her, too. "A training complex of my own will give Harper the stability she needs and I get to keep on doing what I love. It's a win/win."

Cash snagged a water bottle from a nearby cooler and twisted the top. "How far away will you be with your training facility?"

"Nashville," Troy said, wondering if the guy had spoken with Zelda somehow or heard gossip from Isobel. The breakup was so fresh, how would there have been time?

Cash shot a sideways glance his way and said offhandedly, "What about investigating land here?"

What was the purpose of these questions? Just general interest? Surely, he'd spoken of it before. "I chose Nashville so I can cash in to the country music vibe and all the tourists. It's a built-in draw. Launching something like that here would be riskier without the built-in clientele."

"Hmm," Cash said, chugging half of the bottle. "I imagine the start-up costs are higher there, too, the closer you get to the city."

That caught him up short. "I hadn't thought of it that way." Troy eyed Cash suspiciously. "What's really going on here with all these questions?"

Gil and Cash exchanged looks, before Gil said, "We just hate to see you leave."

Cash grabbed two more waters from the cooler, tossing one to Gil, before fixing his bright eyes on Troy and pitching the other plastic bottle his way. "I get that

in the rodeo circuit we see the large and shiny opera-
tions. They certainly have their place and purpose.
But the Top Dog Dude Ranch has shown me how a
smaller organization with a down-to-earth foundation
can flourish." Cash nodded toward the stable. "Here,
we see how keeping the emphasis on the healing power
of the animals speaks louder and brings the best kind
of success."

The guy made it sound so simple, but Troy's practical side still clung to the pages and pages of studies
and number crunches he'd put together for his venture.
Although as he thought about the impressive growth
of the Top Dog Dude Ranch, no question, the trajec-
tory outpaced any he'd studied.

Could he have missed the bigger picture in his
plans? And was it even possible to shift direction this
late in the game? His investor could well see the change
as a lack of focus—if he could even find an appropri-
ate piece of land.

Troy shook his head. "I have more than myself to
consider. Harper's well-being is my responsibility. Although no doubt, eliminating a move would be easier
for her, if I could somehow make things work in this
area."

Cash quirked an eyebrow. "And what do *you* want?"

The question took him aback. He churned the notion around in his brain and finally settled on the core
of the project. "Um, to start a training facility where I
can share my love of rodeo with others."

"Right," Cash pressed. "But do you want to stay
here or go there?"

Put that way, the answer was clear. "I want my daughter to be happy and I want to stay near Zelda."

Putting the words—the wish—out there gave it legs and life beyond when he'd held them inside.

Gil scratched his jaw. "Maybe she would be open to taking a job at the ranch's Nashville-area facility."

"I've mentioned that." Troy thought about that trio of sister houses and the closeness they shared beyond just the placement of those cottages. "She wants to stay near family, especially with Lottie's health concerns."

Even as he said the words, he knew it was more than just that. She was thriving here at the ranch, her spirit healing in a million different ways that shone through her like stars lighting his night.

Her ex had isolated her and then Troy had asked her to relocate as well—a request she's firmly and fairly denied. She deserved to have a relationship where her needs and dreams were prioritized. A relationship with someone who loved her, fully, without reservation.

As he did.

And there was his answer. He loved her. Staying kept him closer to Zelda. Staying was also better for Harper. So one way or another, he needed to find a way to put down roots in Moonlight Ridge, where he could commit himself to winning Zelda's heart.

Zelda blinked back tears, hoping no one would see. Maybe she could claim a stray strand from the horse's mane had gotten into her eye.

Grooming the horses for tomorrow's rodeo should have brought her such joy as she taught Harper how to braid the mane and weave flowers throughout. The artistry of it normally would have made her heart sing.

Except right now, her heart was broken in two.

Using small clear plastic bands from the pockets of her apron, Zelda began dividing the mane of the bay horse. She and Harper worked on two different horses on crossties close to each other.

Splitting the mane between an upper and lower section, her nimble fingers further divided the top part into six chunks. Securing each of the six sections of the top mane with the clear plastic bands, she paused to check on Harper, striding past a pile of delicate artificial flowers—large sets of romantic roses and greenery she'd hot-glued to French barrettes.

The hustle and bustle of other staff prepping for tomorrow's events echoed around them. Each person focused on their task so intently they barely noticed others at work, all moving in a synchronized mayhem.

She leaned to check Harper's work as the girl clipped one of the flower barrettes into the top part of her horse's mane, and noticed a lone tear streaking down her face. Zelda abandoned her own work and rested a hand on Harper's shoulder. "Sweetie, what's wrong?"

Harper shook her head hard, staying silent, working on the braid below the clipped-in flower. Her hands were as unsteady as her breath.

Zelda eased the handful of rubber bands from Harper's fingers. "You can talk to me."

Dealing with someone else's troubles would be a welcome escape from her own.

Harper sagged back against the stall wall, her face puffy and red as she curled her legs to her chest before looking up. In a voice as soft as a light breeze rustling sycamore leaves, she said, "Wynn and I had a fight. Then my dad and I had a fight. Seems like I'm the common denominator in all the arguments."

Zelda slumped against the wall beside her, giving her full attention to Harper. "You've had a rough go of it lately. That can make it all the tougher to hold your tongue."

"That's certainly the truth." She looked at Zelda with red-rimmed eyes and a crumpled attempt at composure. "Just so you know, it's okay if you and my dad are a couple. I know my mom and dad aren't getting remarried. She's probably not even coming home."

Zelda's heart stumbled, her breath too silent as the world closed in around her. How was it possible to feel so much hurt at this belated blessing from Troy's daughter when it could have been such a sweet moment of acceptance? But she didn't think about that for more than a fleeting instant since Harper's feelings were what was most important here.

Harper pushed hair from her face. Strands still clung to the paths tears had formed. "Aren't you going to tell me to keep on hoping?"

Zelda toyed with her paw charm before speaking. "I can't speak for her—or for your father. I can only say that relationships are complicated. And that I'm so very glad your parents were together at least long enough to have you. I wouldn't have missed getting to know you for anything in the world."

The teen looked so despondent, so insecure with all her bravado peeled away. Zelda wanted to sweep her up in a big hug until the hurt faded. "Do you want to talk more about what happened?"

Harper picked up a stray bit of hay, twirling it between her fingers. After an exhale as heavy as summer rain, she looked sidelong at Zelda, lips parting and closing.

Straightening, Harper dusted the hay from her high-rise jeans. "I don't know why I'm so mean to everybody I care about. Wynn, my dad…my mom. I push them all away."

Zelda straightened away from the wall as well and searched for the right words to comfort her during the rare vulnerability. "It's hard sometimes to tell people what we need." She knew well enough from experience. "Then all the frustration just builds and builds until it explodes."

Harper stroked the horse, her breathing evening back out in time with her rhythmic hand. "Even my own mom doesn't want to be around me."

The crux of the girl's pain came sharply into focus. Did Troy even know that Harper didn't blame him? She actually blamed herself.

Hearing the way Harper felt so alone echoed with familiar tones inside Zelda's mind. Hadn't she herself felt utterly and completely isolated earlier in the year? And hadn't at least some of that been of her own making when she'd pushed others away? "Harper, I don't want to say anything negative about your mother, but whatever her reasons for walking away, I can absolutely assure you that you didn't cause it. You are a good kid who's had a lot of change."

Harper ran her fingers through the silky strands of the mane before she started braiding again, seeming calmer than before. "My dad has, too." She bit her bottom lip, more of those tears welling. "I don't know why I keep treating him like garbage."

"Sometimes when we're angry, we lash out at the people we know will stick around no matter what." As the words left her lips, she wondered if she'd transferred her anger and distrust from her past relationship onto Troy. If so, she'd done him a disservice. She didn't know the answer to their long-distance dilemma, but he certainly deserved better than she'd given him breaking things off.

Harper scuffed the toe of her shoe through the dirt. "What do I do about Wynn?"

"Well, you could apologize for the parts that are your fault, and if he doesn't accept responsibility for his portion of the blame, then that tells you all you need to know about him."

"I owe my dad an apology, too."

"I'm sure he would appreciate it."

Harper launched herself forward, hugging Zelda hard. "Thank you. You really are the best."

"Ditto." Zelda hugged her back, her heart squeezing with love for this kid, an affection totally independent from her love for Troy.

Love. For Troy.

The thought stopped her up short, but the truth of it settled inside her with a rightness that surprised her.

She hadn't seen it coming. She certainly hadn't been looking for a relationship. Although she might not even have one left after her argument with Troy.

Perhaps she needed to take her own advice and apologize for her part in the painful discussion. She just prayed she got the sign she needed from him that he cherished her as much as she did him.

Chapter Sixteen

Harper had been practicing her speech all night long, and she hoped she got it just right when she spoke to Wynn. Thanks to Zelda's help, the odds were better. The message clearer.

Now she just needed to find the opportunity in the middle of the events, a festival in full swing outside with rodeo events inside. Making her way toward the arena entrance, she wove around clumps of guests and staff mingling at the different games—horseshoe toss, cornhole and a sack race. A cow-shaped piñata swung from a tree limb, circles of children waiting with wide eyes, each holding a small—empty—candy bag.

Lottie rolled up to take her turn, bat in hand. She swung once, twice, the papier-mâché Holstein busting loose and raining treats. Squealing kids launched forward, scrambling along the ground. It touched her heart to see at least three of the kids pass candy they scooped up to Lottie in her chair.

But best of all, the rodeo.

Proudly wearing her lanyard with a Top Dog Pack staff badge, Harper angled sideways to the front of the line, where she was waved through. Once inside, she scanned the arena, packed full and humming with activity. Staff members darted between groups of riders, checking to make sure they were ready for their events. A mixture of the sweet smell of funnel cake and arena clay filled her nostrils as she scanned the packed bleachers.

Families and teenagers clustered together wearing cowboy hats and boots. From a distance, she could see the connected stable where grooms were rubbing down horses that had already competed in the earlier events. Even above the roar of the crowd as the winner of the roping event was announced, she could hear the horses in the stable whinnying.

Her father stood by the chute, wearing his chaps and holding a clipboard. This was the daddy she grew up with, cheering him and his friends on at events, different counties, but her same "dad." She'd been pretty hard on him lately, and she planned to make that up to him, too.

She found a spot to sit on the edge of a metal bleacher, just as the barrel-racing event began. Her heart pounding faster and faster in her chest, she waited through three participants before finally... Wynn's turn.

Holding her breath, she kept her attention laser-focused on Wynn's minor movements, all the way down to the way he seemed to exhale as he gathered his reins firm in his hand. With a bolt that startled her into breathing again, she watched his bay horse leap forward, kicking the red clay dirt in the air behind him. On the overhead clock, milliseconds ticked by as he turned round the first barrel. Then the next one.

The crowd shot to their feet as he headed for the third and final barrel a good three seconds before the fastest of the previous competitors. Harper jumped, her high-tops reverberating on the metal bleacher floor as Wynn and his bay horse seemed to double their speed when they exited the tight, precise circle around the final barrel.

He really, really was good. Super talented. And she'd seen more than her fair share of cowboys in the ring.

Gathering her courage, she pushed through the crowd, the earthy scents and excited chatter swelling around her. She drew closer to where she'd seen him last and came upon a cluster of girls giggling and asking for his autograph.

Jealousy took a big chomp out of her, like a horse bite. Unexpected and fierce.

"Move aside, ladies," she said, putting an extra oomph in her words. "He's spoken for."

Wynn's eyes went wide with surprise and she hoped he wouldn't deny even knowing her. She counted at least ten heavy heartbeats in her chest, but given her pulse was so rapid, it may not have been much time.

His smile wide, he extended his hand. "Hey, Harper. Glad you could make it."

With relief, she noticed the genuine warmth in his eyes, a pleasure she felt sure he wouldn't fake.

She linked her fingers with his, following him as he tucked into a corner, half shielded from the crowd by a stack of hay bales. Her stomach fluttered with nerves as she rolled out an apology, and prayed he would meet her halfway, as Zelda said he should. "I'm sorry it didn't work out for us. And I'm really sorry I wasn't kinder with my words."

He squeezed her hand, his handsome face so kind. "We've both had a lot of tough stuff thrown at us by life. Probably for the best we sort that out, huh?"

His words were just what she would have hoped for, what Zelda said they should be.

"Yeah," she acknowledged, shyly looking at the arena clay on her high-tops before meeting his eyes, "but I want you to know, you're the coolest, smartest guy I've ever met."

"Not so much the smartest," he said with a wince, his gaze skipping toward the stable for a moment before shifting back to her. Even in the warm glow of the overhead lights, she saw him grow pale.

Could it be that he was just as insecure about some stuff as she was? She'd been so wrapped up in his rodeo-star quality—so mired in her own misery— she'd missed really hearing him.

"Hey," she said, resting a hand on his shoulder, "you shouldn't put yourself down like that. Don't you know that it takes more than brawn to win in the ring that way? You gotta think fast on your feet. That's a fierce brand of smarts."

"I never thought of it that way," he said, his voice full of surprise and an earnest hopefulness that tugged at her.

"Well, think on it from now on," she retorted with a smile and a firmness she hoped he took to heart. "And just so you know, I heard what you said about my dad being a stand-up guy."

"I'm glad." Wynn grinned, his charm reaching out to her all over again like when she'd first seen him. "Do you mind if I call you after I go home?"

Happiness bloomed inside her, filling every corner. She arched to give him a kiss on the cheek and said, "I'd like that. A lot." She clasped both his hands in hers and backed toward the road. "But don't forget, we've still got plenty rodeoing and partying to enjoy here before you go."

Back during her days in Atlanta, Zelda had yearned for large, wonderfully noisy evenings like this. The party barn was packed to the brim for the saloon-themed gala, a celebration for the adults after the rodeo. But tonight, her heart was too heavy and conflicted to enjoy the festivities, searching for Troy and wondering if there could possibly be a way through their differences. A way that her love for him could grow and he would return the feelings in equal measure.

As she approached the barn, the tinny sound of an old piano blended with a banjo and fiddle playing modern country tunes with a throwback twist. She needed to shake off her personal feelings before she entered the party. To help lift her mood, she thought about the big hug Harper had given her after their talk the day before. Even if things were over for good between Troy and Zelda, she would know she helped his daughter at a critical time and that felt good. Harper had helped her, too, in so many ways this summer, and Zelda would always be grateful. With that in mind, she was able to shake off a little of her sadness.

She smoothed her hands down her costume, a steampunk vibe dress, with black taffeta and fishnet stockings. She'd chosen the edgy getup earlier in the week, delighting at the prospect of seeing Troy's face light up.

Now? She wouldn't have stayed at all, but her boss had strongly encouraged participation. And since they'd officially offered her a full-time, year-round position as head of the grooming salon, she was obligated to schmooze with the guests even when her heart was breaking.

Pushing through the swinging saloon doors, she entered what felt like a step back in time. Footsteps stomped along the planked stage with line dancers. The stable manager sat on top of the upright piano, wearing a barmaid dress and singing. Sepia-tone wanted posters lined a wall, sporting photos of the Top Dog Dude Ranch staff. In the only nod to modern technology, television screens were hung in all four corners, running video footage from the rodeo and camp.

An image filled the monitor of Wynn holding a trophy, followed by another of him and Harper sitting on a picnic blanket. She would have thought it an old video clip if not for the trophy resting on the quilt.

Happiness for Harper glowed inside her. She had spoken to her briefly after the rodeo, and the teen had made a point of thanking her for the advice. It had been a simple, sweet exchange, and in that moment, Zelda's heart had filled with love for the girl. Now, a deep relief joined that love, as the teens seemed to have found their way to a happier farewell.

A deep lump formed in her throat. What if she couldn't find a reconciliation of her own with Troy? She would miss Harper so deeply as well.

Winging another prayer for that much-needed sign, Zelda adjusted her top hat—decorated with silver chains and metallic watch gears—and searched for her sisters. They'd intended to walk over together. But Isobel had been delayed by a last-minute phone call, and Neve had lost track of time during a nature walk.

Angling past a wooden stand marked Moonshine and Munchies, she spotted familiar faces—Cash dressed as a lumberjack and Gil as a miner—but just as soon they disappeared from sight into the sea of Stetsons and chaps.

A tap on her shoulder startled her into turning around.

"Isobel," she gasped, "there you are."

Although she was almost unrecognizable, sporting a gingham dress and bonnet that looked straight out of *Little House on the Prairie*. Neve drew up beside her, prim and buttoned up in her schoolmarm costume.

Isobel clasped her hand in a tight grip and drew her from the crowd, tucking away in a corner beside a carved bear statue. "I have the most exciting news." She trembled so hard her bonnet fell back off her head, hanging from the strings around her neck. "We got a hit on a donor match, a closer match than even the one prior who got mono."

Zelda clapped a hand over her heart, and even

though her leather bustier wasn't laced that tight, she could barely breathe. "That's incredible news. But isn't that fast from just this afternoon? I thought the results took a week or so."

Isobel tugged her bonnet off impatiently and continued, "The person isn't from today's sign-up. It's someone who got tested last week. I can hardly believe it. I was so devastated when the other donor got sick. Little did I know it would give us time to find an even better one. A closer match."

Neve tipped her head to the side, nudging her tiny steel-rimmed glasses. "Do you know who it is? Is he or she someone local or from far away?"

Isobel's eyes lit with delight, her smile secretive. "A man. Early sixties. Local."

The age and gender settled in her mind, lining up with the time frames they'd searched in local records. Could it possibly be…

Zelda touched her chest over her racing heart. "Do think he might be Gran's son? The age is right."

Isobel spread her arms and shrugged, the bonnet dangling from her fingers. "It's possible and something to look into soon. Right now, I can only think of Lottie. I'm just so relieved I can hardly string any thoughts together beyond what this means for my daughter." She chewed her bottom lip for a moment before taking a breath. "Prepare yourself, because you've met him. He's been right here under our noses all along. It's River Jack Hadley."

Zelda's knees folded and she sat on an aged whiskey barrel. "The jewelry maker. It's like kismet."

Neve pressed a hand over the silver watch pin attached to her bodice. "Strange, because if I recall correctly, his son Gil wasn't at all a match."

"I asked the same question when I spoke with River Jack an hour ago," Isobel said promptly. "He was thrilled to be a match for Lottie and reassured me he is on board with the procedure. Then he also told me that Gil is adopted, and River Jack opted for adoption because he himself was adopted."

Zelda reeled with the news. The man could really and truly be Gran's son.

Cautiously optimistic, she scanned the crowd, her gaze landing on River Jack, dressed appropriately in a miner's costume. She searched his face for signs of kinship, hints of Gran's features. But beyond a dimple in his chin, she just couldn't be sure.

This certainly wasn't the time to bring up Gran's will to him. Uncovering an adoption history was delicate and personal. Although they'd been so vocal about their search, could River Jack have possibly already guessed?

Either way, they'd succeeded in their most important quest of all, securing a healthier future for Lottie. Nothing mattered more than that. And there was hope on the horizon for fulfilling Gran's dying wish that her crystal ring could be given to her long-lost child.

Relief surged through her, and she yearned to share all of the happy news with Troy. She could hear in her mind how he would whoop for joy and sweep her up into his arms, spinning her around. She couldn't stop herself from scanning the room again, this time searching for his broad shoulders and ruggedly handsome face.

Neve shoulder-bumped her, pointing toward the piano. "Look. Isn't that Troy?"

Her breath hitching, Zelda searched and found him taking the microphone from the singer on top of the piano. He tapped the mic twice, drawing all eyes toward him.

Not that Zelda needed any enticement to take in the sight of him in his jeans and chaps, but also wearing spurs and a ten-gallon hat.

"Good evening, everyone," Troy said, his voice deep and commanding. "Thank you all for your support in making today's event such a huge success for the youth and our community."

Applause echoed up to the soaring barn roof, then settled as he continued, "I would like to take a moment to thank one of our unsung behind-the-scenes leaders. Someone who brought an added beauty and caring to our rugged sport. Now, I invite you to turn your attention to the video screens for a short presentation featuring the artistry of our groomer, Zelda Dalton."

Her heart thudded as he shared the spotlight with her. Zelda pointed to herself in shock, mouthing the words, "Who, me?"

From across the room, Troy nodded, sweeping his hat off and bowing in her direction. Standing again, he motioned toward the screen in the nearest corner.

Images flickered of her weaving flowers through Lyra's mane. Another highlighted her plaiting a horse's tail, with ribbons woven through. Then a short clip featured her training Harper how to secure tiny blossoms through multiple tiny braids. He'd even showcased a few brief snippets of her in the salon, sprucing up dogs and even flinging bubbles back and forth with Harper.

Beside her, Neve squeezed her hand. Isobel gave a romantic sigh of approval.

Tears burned behind her eyes as Zelda thought back to her conversation with Troy where she'd lauded her sisters' talents and he reminded her of her artistry with animals. The video showed he hadn't just been spouting platitudes. She saw herself through his eyes.

Felt how he valued her.

She'd been looking for a sign that he understood her, saw her, could be willing to meet her halfway in an equal partnership with the possibility of a future. As far as signs went, this one set a gold standard. His thoughtfulness was everything she could have imagined from the man of her dreams, the love of her life.

And just what she needed to give her hope that working together, they could forge a path forward.

Troy strode across the barn, shouldering past the partiers congratulating him on the rodeo. While the band returned to their instruments, he kept his gaze laser-focused on Zelda standing with her sisters, a carved bear looming behind her like a warning not to break her heart.

He certainly intended to try his best to treat her feelings with the tenderest of care.

Through the video, he had watched Zelda's face from across the room and he hoped—prayed—he hadn't misread the signs of her happiness. But even if his gesture with the presentation about her grooming art wasn't enough to convince her of his intentions, he wouldn't give up. Zelda deserved it all—the romance, the devotion and whatever else her heart desired.

And—what do you know?—love for Zelda was turning him into a diehard romantic.

Edging around a card table full of guests trying their hand at Texas Hold'em, he stopped in front of the sibling trio, with eyes only for Zelda. He had to admit, her costume had his pulse racing from her spike-heeled boots to the steam-punk top hat perched on her head, her long braid draped over her shoulder.

"Ladies," he said, sweeping his ten-gallon hat from his head. "I hope you won't mind if I steal this stunning saloon girl away from you for a walk under the stars."

Isobel twirled her prairie bonnet by the strings. "Of course not."

Neve gave a wink that was far from that of a prim schoolmarm. "Y'all behave now."

Extending a hand, he left the final decision up to Zelda. His chest went tight with last-minute nerves. Thank heaven she didn't make him wait for long.

Zelda clasped his fingers, tucking close to his side. Her vanilla scent filled his senses as her smile filled his heart.

"Lead the way," she said without hesitation or doubt.

Relief wracked through him and he gave her hand a squeeze as he led her toward the open barn doors, stepping outside, where they could speak privately. He'd given a lot of thought to this part of his plan, even though he'd been far from certain of her agreement to listen.

He led her past the party barn, deeper into the woods, music from the gala growing softer, hoot owls and bullfrogs growing louder.

She tipped her face toward him, moonlight streaming down over her flushed cheeks. "Did you hear? They've found a donor for Lottie."

"Really?" he asked in surprise, but so very thankful. "Already?"

"Apparently it was someone who got tested last week and the results came in late today." She drew in a breath, then whispered, "It's River Jack Hadley."

He let out a little whistle, thrilled at the news.

"No kidding. Right here under our noses the whole time," he said with an ironic chuckle. Steering her toward a particular spot he had in mind. "That's fantastic."

"An incredible relief for all of us." She stepped gingerly over a log as he braced a steadying palm on her spine. "I can't believe you did all that for me with the video."

"I was only showcasing your work and your generosity. Most of all, your heart. You make everything you touch beautiful and it was my joy to share that with everyone tonight." He stopped her with a gentle hand and pointed toward their destination, an oak tree by a pond.

Early this morning, he'd hung a large porch swing from a sprawling branch, then arranged for the ranch's landscaper and Harper to decorate it with flowers along the ropes. Electric lanterns were draped along the limbs.

She gasped in surprise, her eyes filling with tears as she took it all in. "You did this? For me? I don't know what to say."

She didn't have to. Her expression said so much. He was glad he'd managed to surprise her. Please her.

Gently, he guided her toward the swing.

"You don't need to say a word. In fact, there are things I want to tell you first." He waited until she sat, and then he took his place beside her, where he hoped he would have the right to stay for the rest of his life. "I'm not leaving Moonlight Ridge."

The swing swayed and settled, branches rustling overhead, beams from the strings of lights dancing along the earth.

"I don't understand." Her eyes went wide, her forehead pinched with worry. "Did something fall through with the training center?"

He'd done a significant amount of reevaluating since their argument. He just hoped she agreed. Even if she didn't, he knew his new direction was grounded in the values he held close.

"Nothing fell through," he explained, gathering his words for the most important pitch of his life—winning Zelda's heart. "I rethought my priorities and that reshaped my plan. I'm going to suggest a new location to Levi, one here in Moonlight Ridge. It will be more remote than the previous acreage, but with a down-to-earth, more intimate vibe like here at the

Top Dog Dude Ranch—something Levi noted on more than one occasion."

"That sounds wonderful," she said in a cautiously hopeful voice. "But what if he doesn't agree? I thought this was important for Harper, too?"

He'd once thought opening the training center was the most critical goal in his life. Now he knew otherwise. Building a future with Zelda, Harper and Maisey—even other children and four-legged family members—mattered most.

But he didn't want to scare Zelda off, so he eased into his thoughts. "Harper needs stability and security. If my idea for a facility in Moonlight Ridge doesn't work out, Jacob has already offered me a job at the ranch more than once, an open-ended invitation, according to him."

"Are you sure that's what you want?" She leaned closer, such joy shining in her eyes, he couldn't possibly miss her happiness at his decision.

Another bolt of relief shot through him. "Absolutely. I realized I was looking at the training center in the wrong light. I was envisioning it as a replacement for the excitement of the rodeo circuit, and I was missing what it should be—until the Top Dog Dude Ranch helped me refocus on my priorities."

"And those are?" Her smile encouraged him.

"Family. Healing. Connecting to the people around us. And again, family."

"I like that." She leaned into him, the swing swaying gently, a couple of leaves whispering down. "It's certainly what I've found to be true since coming here and rediscovering my family."

He took her hand and clasped it lightly. Gratefully. "Most of all, I want *you*."

She opened her mouth and he rested a finger over her lips. He needed to be the one to say the words first. They'd been chasing around his head nonstop ever since the moment he'd learned the truth of his feelings.

"Because, Zelda Dalton, I love you with all my heart and I want nothing more than to remind you of that every day for the rest of my life."

He felt the vow to the depth of his being.

She kissed the tip of his finger, then clasped his wrist to move aside his touch. She pressed her mouth to his and whispered, "I have fallen totally and completely in love with you, Troy. You swept me off my feet from that very first day and I can't wait to see what adventures life has in store for us next."

With a whoop of joy that resonated all the way to his soul, he swept her hat from her head and slid his fingers under her braid, drawing her into his arms for now…and always.

* * * * *